VICTORIA'S SIX

BROTHERHOOD PROTECTORS WORLD

DELILAH DEVLIN

VICTORIA'S SIX

ATHENA PROJECT BOOK #2

New York Times & *USA Today*
Bestselling Author

Delilah Devlin

CHAPTER 1

A HARD SHOULDER butted against her belly, taking away her breath. Not that her adversary today had given her the full might of his movement. Still, he managed to fold her over that hard shoulder as he straightened and swept her off her feet. As she sailed behind him, she forced herself to go with it instead of tensing in anticipation, tucking in her chin before landing. Her surrender to the move lessened the impact when her back slapped the mat.

Dragging in a deep breath, Victoria Cross gave her sparring partner a stern glare. "You could've warned me we were starting again."

He arched an eyebrow.

Yeah, that had been the point. He'd wanted to surprise her and check out *her* moves. He'd already made his opinion of her fitness for close-in, hand-to-hand combat measures perfectly clear. If they ever faced that sort of attack, she was to let him lead. Step behind him. Let his superior size and strength take the lead. Always.

Logically, she could see the sense of it. He was an ex-SEAL, built big and tall, not an ounce of lazy flab on his muscular frame. At thirty-seven, he was still in his prime. Battle-hardened.

And dear Lord was he hard.

Shoving that thought aside, she accepted the hand he offered her and let him pull her up in front of him. "You were holding back," she said, frowning. Something that irritated the shit out of her because it was becoming a pattern. One she was trying to break because he needed to learn to trust in her skills and abilities.

"I used an appropriate amount of force," he said, one corner of his mouth kicking up.

That half-smile and the deliberate deepening of his southern drawl had her seeing red—he was patronizing "the little woman." She shot out both hands, slamming them against his chest while at the same time sweeping out a foot to catch him behind the ankles.

He didn't budge.

She'd used the same move when sparring with her last partner and had planted his butt on the mat numerous times.

Logan Tackett sighed, gripped one of her arms,

and turned her, folding her into his embrace so tightly she couldn't use her elbows to strike his gut. Further, he quickly kicked out and hooked a leg around her ankles, preventing her from stomping on his foot. He had her completely trapped and under his control.

His head lowered, and he spoke into her ear. "You done?"

Seeing as they'd already spent an hour beating punching bags and each other, she relaxed, glad none of her friends were there to see her so over-matched. They'd have laughed themselves silly. "You can let me go now."

"You sure?" he asked, his breath stirring the hair sticking to her cheek that had come loose from her ponytail.

"We have a meeting with Jake Cogburn in the conference room," she reminded him while gritting her teeth.

His leg released hers. His arms fell away. When he stepped back from her, she felt a stirring of cool air against her sweaty back and strangely missed his warmth. "I'm heading to the shower," she said. "See you at the meeting." Then she quickly moved away, trying to leave behind some conflicting feel-ings—irritation with herself for not meeting the moment because she'd been working hard to earn his respect and disappointment that he'd let her go.

That last realization had her shaking her head.

Logan was her partner. She'd never go *there*. Besides, she'd noted that he tended to have some old-fashioned views about a woman's place in this organization. He'd be fine with her if she kept to her lane—something she'd never accept.

All the while she showered and changed, she worked on clearing her mind and assuming her usual calm, professional aplomb. She wondered what the meeting was about. Maybe she and Logan were going to catch their first solo mission, which should've pleased her, but she worried about working with him while he wasn't fully invested with the concept of having a true partner. He'd likely think of her as his backup while he led, and she wasn't having it.

To add to her ambivalence regarding her new job, Victoria wasn't all that eager to begin work with a new employer. Before arriving in Colorado, she'd finished a months-long sting, working undercover for the FBI to expose and prosecute a sex trafficking ring that had operated on the East Coast and had been run by an Eastern European crime syndicate. She'd worked in a strip club as a dancer and beer bitch, cozying up to the mob boss, who, thankfully, had run a "clean" club. He'd been smarter than the average Russian mafia boss, wanting to run his club under the radar so the real business could stay hidden, which was why it had taken her and her partner, who'd tended bar there, so long to get the goods on the organization.

After so many months of sliding into that underworld, she needed time to breathe fresher air and recoup. Time to let the scum slough off her skin. After that job, which had taken far too long and had ended horrendously, with her partner grievously wounded and herself a second away from joining his fate, she'd been more than ready to hand in her resignation and look for something else to do.

She'd thought she'd have plenty of time for some relaxation. Her pay had accumulated into a healthy nest egg since she'd had to live off her meager wages and tips from her undercover job.

However, her best friend, former CIA-operative Rebecca "Beck" Morrissey, had left messages on the cellphone Victoria had kept in a locker while she'd been on assignment. Over thirty messages. The last one telling her to get her ass on a plane to Wyoming. So, Victoria had handed her resignation to her handler, telling him she was taking two months of termination leave she'd accumulated and wouldn't be back. Then she'd boarded a plane, heading to Wyoming for a training seminar.

It was the last thing in the world Victoria had wanted to do, but after Beck had told her that some old friends, a group of women from across various government agencies, who'd met during interagency operations or through friends of friends, like Beck, she couldn't turn her down. It sounded like fun. A chance to kick back and catch up with friends, women who understood the kind of life she'd led.

Only, the training seminar had turned into a search to find Beck's sister, Leslie, who'd been kidnapped by right-wing wingnuts. Along the way, she'd been briefed by Beck about what she had in mind, teaming up with their friends, who were also burned out and ready to do something else. Before the seminar had begun, they'd kicked around the idea of opening their own agency, but Beck had a friend, Hank Patterson, who ran the Brotherhood Protectors out of Montana, and she was thinking, maybe, they could skip the headache of building an organization from the ground up and simply throw in with Hank to form their own task group inside Hank's Protectors.

After the women had proven their capabilities by being part of the team that had not only rescued Beck's sister but had also brought down a domestic terrorist group, Hank had invited them to join his organization. They'd be working paired with male operators, the same ones they'd teamed up with while hunting for Leslie.

Now, Victoria was part of the newly formed Athena Project, and her new partner was Logan Tackett. In another lifetime, Victoria might have liked working with the handsome former SEAL. Logan was over six feet tall and had dark brown hair and gray eyes. His burly, muscular build was just her type—if she was looking for a hook-up—but she wasn't ready for another *partner* and didn't want the responsibility of keeping him safe—despite his unshakeable belief that their roles were reversed.

Sure, he was a former SEAL and could handle himself, but her last partner had been ex-Special Forces and hadn't managed to dodge a bullet.

Plus, Logan seemed to think that he needed to watch out for her just because she was pretty and slim. When they'd been searching for signs of Leslie in the Wind River Mountains, he'd been the one to drive the ATV along the steep dirt trails. She hadn't bothered griping at him about it; his action had left her hands free in case she'd had to draw the weapon strapped to her thigh.

Not that she'd shared her reasons for letting him get his way—which might have proven to be a mistake. She'd forgotten the old maxim of beginning something the way you intended it to go forward.

Renewed after her shower and now dressed in jeans, boots, and a waffle-knit Henley shirt, she made her way into the vacation lodge's basement where the Colorado branch of the Brotherhood Protectors was located.

Pushing through the door of the conference room, she pulled up short when she noted that Hank Patterson, the head honcho over the entire organization, and his movie-star wife, Sadie McClain, were seated at the table, along with Jake and Beck—and Logan, who'd managed to beat her to the meeting.

He reached out to push back the chair next to him as she approached.

"You know everyone here…?" Jake began.

She nodded and took the seat next to Logan.

Hank turned to Sadie. "This is all yours, sweetheart."

Sadie smiled at him then turned toward Logan and Victoria.

Victoria sucked in a quick breath because Sadie's smile alone was worth a million dollars. The blonde was simply stunning.

"I have a project that starts filming in a week." She waved a hand and shook her head. "Not that it's important, but I'm the lead and Harlie James is playing my little sister. A comedy of sorts. The little sister is a bit of a wild child, and I have to rush in to save her from her own bad decisions." She leaned forward. "Well, the casting director and co-producer couldn't have chosen a more perfect actress to play my wild child sister. Harlie is that and more. The thing is," she said, wrinkling her nose, "I'm also an executive producer for the movie, and the company providing insurance for the film, to include covering the stars, is balking at covering Harlie. They don't trust that she won't do something to jeopardize our starting date."

Victoria had no idea where the woman was going with this. She glanced at Logan and saw that he, too, was frowning.

"What Sadie would get to if I gave her the rest of the day," Hank said, a grin stretching his mouth, "is that we need someone to babysit Harlie until she arrives on set."

"You need a babysitter?" Logan asked. "I mean, all we have to do is follow her around and make sure she doesn't trip in her high heels?"

Sadie laughed. "Oh, if only it would be that easy. You see, Harlie's a bit of an adrenaline junkie. If you look at her Instagram, you'll see that in just the past month, she's been zip-lining in Costa Rica, whitewater rafting on the Snake River…" She shook her head. "When she was required to see the production company's doctor for a physical, he said she had a hairline fracture on her wrist and various bruises—okay, maybe those don't seem like a big deal, but when you're facing millions of dollars of losses if you delay filming, well, we can't afford that. She has to stay safe, wrapped up in cotton wool…"

"You can't order her to sit on some beach and do nothing?" Victoria asked.

"We tried. She says she completely understands our concerns, but she's got this big party planned. She's already rented an estate, invited all her friends, including the male lead of our film, and she's not willing to cancel. She'd be out too much money."

"A party..." Victoria still didn't see the problem.

"The party," Sadie said, leaning over the table, "is on a ranch outside of Jackson Hole. A dude ranch that caters to the wealthy. And not the kind that offers rides on old hack horses—they advertise ATV adventures in the mountains, sky-diving into remote areas for long hikes back—"

"Bronc-busting," Hank said, shaking his head.

"How many days is this party?" Logan asked.

"Five."

"And all you want us to do is sit on her?" Victoria asked.

Sadie sighed and sat back, a smile on her lips that looked a bit crimped. Her expression was so hopeful that Victoria blinked and forced herself not to shake her head.

"It should be an easy job," Hank said, and then he told them how much the production company was willing to pay them.

Victoria felt her jaw sag just a little.

"Like Hank said, it should be easy," Sadie said, then winced. "And Harlie's a sweetheart..."

"But..." Victoria mumbled.

"She's…excitable. Once she gets an idea in her head, she drags everyone else along with her enthusiasm. And it's nigh unto impossible to put the brakes on her…adventures…when she gets like that."

Logan straightened his shoulders. "I'm sure we can handle one little actress."

Sadie's perfectly arched eyebrows shot upward.

Victoria felt her own back bristle at his masculine arrogance. "When will we be needed?"

Hank pushed a large envelope across the table. "The company's jet will fly you to Jackson Hole tonight. There's a dossier on Harlie, cash for incidentals and wardrobe—"

"Wardrobe?" Logan asked.

"You're posing as house party guests. Taking my spots," Sadie said. "She might balk if she thought we were sending someone to supervise her. I've told her I can't get away, but I'm sending a production company rep, who needs a reward for all his hard work getting ready for filming—and his girlfriend. You'll need a wardrobe to fit in with the party's theme."

"Theme?"

Victoria didn't blame Logan for his confusion or monosyllabic questions. She was feeling a little dazed at the moment, too. They were leaving tonight?

"It's a dude ranch. You'll need appropriate

clothing, including cowboy hats and boots. There will be a couple of parties, so you might need something blingy to wear to fit in. There's a heated swimming pool—so swimwear…" Sadie checked her diamond-encrusted watch. "I've included the addresses of a couple of stores in Colorado Springs that should see to all your needs."

Jake grinned across the table at them. "Better get a move on."

Logan glanced at him, and his eyes narrowed.

Victoria looked at Hank. "So, it's undercover… because we don't want our target to be aware we're protecting her? We're protecting her from herself? No bad guys?"

Hank grimaced. "Didn't say that…"

"We've had some incidents on the set already," Sadie said. "They might have just been caused by careless workers—"

"Or sabotage," Hank said, giving her a frown.

"Why would anyone want to sabotage the set?" Logan asked.

Hank sighed. "Harlie got herself into a little trouble with a former boyfriend."

"A member of the Saudi royal family," Sadie added.

"An unsavory businessman *attached* to the royal family," Hank corrected. "He wanted to marry her, but she tried to put the skids on their relationship. She says she thinks he tried to have her abducted from Costa Rica when she went there for some ziplining and deep-sea diving." He pointed at the dossier. "Our tech guy, Swede, worked up a profile on him, too."

Logan looked a little less affronted by the thought that there might be a "real" mission. Victoria looked to Beck. Her expression didn't give away much, but her eyes glinted with humor.

Victoria subtly shook her head at her friend, knowing Beck had been the one to saddle her with this assignment.

"I guess that's everything," Hank said and pushed up from the table. Everyone else stood as well. "We'll be heading back to Montana. We'll have a fresh pilot here tonight for your trip." He held out his hand across the table. Logan and Victoria shook hands then remained standing.

"Good luck to both of you." From the look on Hank's face, he thought they'd need it.

When the couple had left, Victoria planted her hands on her hips and glared balefully at Beck. "Seriously?"

Beck chuckled. "It's some *serious* money."

"I was hoping for a *serious* job."

"You don't think it is?" Jake asked, the corners of his mouth twitching.

Yeah, the man was in charge of the Colorado branch, but Victoria didn't care. "We're babysitting.

Do you know how over-qualified we are for this assignment?"

Jake glanced between Logan and her. "Yes, it should be an easy assignment to keep her out of trouble. However, I figured the two of you needed to do something…low-key…so you can find your footing as a team. From what I've seen, neither of you has settled into your roles as partners. There's been some friction."

He'd noticed? Had everyone seen it? She glanced at Beck, who gave her a nod.

Well, shit. No one had ever accused her of being unprofessional, and Jake hadn't. Not yet, anyway. She blew out a breath and turned to Logan. "Maybe they're right."

Logan's mouth tightened, and then he shrugged. "I haven't had any issues workin' with you other than the fact you have a hard time takin' orders."

Beck coughed.

Jake's face screwed up into a grimace. "That's what you both need to work on. You're partners. You have to trust each other—and it's not just on her side, man."

Logan frowned, and when his gaze swung back to her, she noted that his gray eyes looked almost silver when he was scowling.

She picked up the packet from the table, lifted her chin, and gave him a dazzling Sadie-style smile.

"Well, *darlin'*," she said, her voice dripping with honey, "we have some shopping to do."

Logan grunted, grabbed her hand, and settled it into the crook of his elbow. "*Sweetheart,* just make sure you find somethin' sexy to wear for when we're alone…"

Then he pulled her along toward the door while laughter sounded from the pair they left behind. With heat filling her cheeks, Victoria decided to accept his challenge. In fact, she'd make sure that Logan didn't take any of the many assets she brought to their partnership for granted. This assignment might be fun, after all.

CHAPTER 2

Logan stood near the counter of the pricey women's store, checking his watch for the twentieth time. Their trip to the western store hadn't taken long, and Victoria hadn't made him wait more than half an hour as she'd selected boots, a hat, numerous pairs of jeans, and snap-button western shirts. He'd actually admired how efficiently she'd attacked the list of items she'd drawn up during their drive to Colorado Springs.

Two hours ago, he'd dropped her at the women's shop while he'd hit a men's store, looking for sports jackets, slacks, and shoes. He'd been surprised when he'd entered and a sales associate had greeted him, telling him that Ms. McClain had already phoned and told him everything Logan would need for evening wear. Logan hadn't balked at any of the suggestions and had been grateful for the streamlined process.

He'd hoped to get back to the lodge at Fool's Gold with time to spare for packing and maybe a workout, but apparently, Victoria was a bit choosier about her clothing purchases than he'd been. From the women moving in and out of the dressing room area, their arms filled with colorful items, he figured he might be waiting until well past "wheels up"—not that the plane would really leave without them. Still, he was more than a little annoyed.

"This is so exciting," the woman behind the counter bubbled.

The blonde had been trying to engage him in a conversation since he'd arrived, but he wasn't in the mood for it. Sure, he was polite and had accepted a coffee when she'd offered it, but she was very young and a bit starstruck by the idea of helping out Sadie McClain's "Hollywood friends." Her enthusiasm was a bit draining.

He glanced toward the dressing rooms, and his jaw sagged for a fraction of a second until he clamped it closed. Victoria was standing in front of mirrors, two associates flanking her. Her dark brown hair was mussed, and her cheeks were rosy as she scrutinized her reflection. The black dress she wore had full-length sleeves and hugged her slim body from her shoulders to the tops of her thighs where the hem ended. His gaze swept her bare legs, which were long and nicely curved. The best set he'd ever seen. When his gaze moseyed back up, it collided with hers in the mirror.

Her eyebrows were lowered, and her mouth was crimped.

Busted! He pulled his gaze away and tried to pretend nonchalance after being caught ogling his partner. But damn! He'd seen her in bike shorts, had placed his hands on her body when they'd sparred, but seeing her in that dress hit home the fact she was a beautiful woman, and now, he wished he hadn't noticed because they were working together and a man didn't shit in his own backyard. And now he was smacking himself internally for thinking anything so crass even if he hadn't said it out loud.

He took another sip of his coffee and winced, forgetting it was hot. It was just as well the roof of his mouth was scalded. Served him right. It'd give him something to think about other than the way her dark eyebrows had formed wings over her brown eyes when she'd frowned at him. Damn, she looked hot.

Good Lord, a scalded mouth wasn't enough of a distraction. All he could think about was the fact they'd be pretending to be a couple for five days. He'd never had a female partner before, and that fact felt like a bit of a handicap. He always seemed to say or do the wrong thing around her. When they'd worked out, trying to learn each other's moves and strengths, he'd held back, not wanting to hurt her—and had she thanked him? Hell, no.

He could still remember her frown when she'd scolded him for going easy on her. He was two hundred pounds—if he landed on her, she'd snap like a twig. What had she expected?

At last, one of the saleswomen strode to the counter with a stack of items, which she told the blonde to ring up at the register. A few minutes later, Victoria joined him after changing back into her jeans and long-sleeve shirt.

Victoria held up a hand. "I don't want to hear it. I know you've been waiting far too long." She wrinkled her nose. "Sadie sent suggestions, and those women were efficient, but seriously, how many outfits am I really going to need? Glad I'm not paying the bill."

He smirked and leaned toward her. "Might want to save the tags. Do you think we'll have to return the clothes when we get back?"

She laughed and shook her head. "According to Sadie's instructions, I was to choose what pleased me and consider everything a gift from her since we're doing her such a big favor."

"Guess we'll find out how big a favor it is when we get there," he muttered, glad she seemed to be in a good mood now.

The blonde rang up the clothes while another folded and wrapped the items in tissue paper before settling them into three big bags—one completely devoted to shoes.

When they were back in his vehicle, Logan sighed and stretched out his shoulders.

"Yeah, it's going to be a long night," she said, sighing.

"It's good we're both stayin' at the lodge, so packin' our bags will be quick. Maybe we can catch some shuteye on the plane. We'll have to recon the place as soon as we get there."

"Without anyone realizing that's what we're doing…"

"I don't know how that's gonna work."

She chuckled. "All I can think is that we'll be spending lots of time pretending like we're necking if anyone comes close."

Logan tried to see the downside. He really did. He cleared his throat. "I've never worked with a female. I mean, in the Navy there were females, sure, but not with us on missions—unless they were pilots or spooks."

"Just think of me as one of the guys," she said airily.

When he shot her a look, he found she was grinning.

"See?" she said. "Is it so hard to admit you don't have a clue how to move forward?"

"I have a clue. This is a mission, like any other. It's just…"

She tsked. "Logan, Logan, Logan… If it helps, pretend I don't have boobs or that you outweigh me by eighty pounds. Expect the same from me that you'd get from any one of the other Protectors."

He snorted. "How you gonna hide your weapon when you're wearin' that skimpy little black dress? Think you'll have time to run back to your room to get it if shit goes south?"

"Do you mean *our* room?"

He blinked and shot her another glance. "What?"

"I see I'm going to be the brains of this partner-ship," she drawled. "Didn't you read Sadie's note inside that envelope? We're sharing a room. We're a couple, remember?"

"Oh, fuck." Sharing a room? His mind went straight to the gutter again.

"Yeah, that's a word you can forget."

"Sorry, what word?"

"Fuck. There will be none of that," she grum-bled. "We're partners. Both adults, or at least, I am. We can share a room."

She sounded like she was trying to convince herself that was true. From her frown and the way she crossed her arms in front of her chest, she was throwing up any defenses she could against the very idea they'd be living together in close quarters.

"Think they did this on purpose?" he asked. "Since it seems they noticed we've had some trouble adjustin' to workin' together?"

"They're probably laughing their asses off." She settled lower in her seat. "We'll just have to work like a well-oiled team and show them how wrong they are."

"Well-oiled" wasn't a word he wanted in his brain when he thought about working with her. "You know we're gonna have to practice some to pull off bein' boyfriend and girlfriend. And come up with some couple code."

"What do you mean?"

"You'll need to get used to me touchin' you. You'll have to touch me. We'll need to practice kissin', so we know which way we lean and don't bump noses. And we'll need a history—when and where we met, how long we've been datin', where we live, cats or dogs, beaches or mountains… Shit like that."

She laughed. "You think we need to practice kissing?"

That was the only part she'd heard? His mouth curved. It was good knowing she was just as aware of him as he was of her. Now, he wouldn't worry so much about hiding his…uh, *admiration* for the assets she brought to the team.

. . .

VICTORIA REARRANGED the blanket their flight attendant had provided when they had boarded the small private jet. She sat in a chair that adjusted backward and had a footrest, so she could actually "catch some shuteye" like Logan was somehow managing to do quite well.

He sat opposite her, just the narrow aisle between them.

She hadn't missed the looks the woman who'd served them a light dinner had given him. She'd admired every inch of him, head to toe, and she'd given him much warmer smiles than she'd given to Victoria. When the woman had left, dimming the cabin lights, Logan had glanced across the aisle and given her a wink, so she knew he was aware that the woman had been flirting—and that she'd noticed.

Well, she couldn't really blame the woman. Even asleep, with his jaw sagging, the man was fine. All male. Lean and muscled.

Victoria closed her eyes and tried to sleep. She knew she'd need it. They'd hit the ground running, trying to get a handle on the woman they'd been sent to protect. Somehow, they'd have to find a way to ingratiate themselves into her inner circle of friends for the weekend.

Logan had his "in" if he used it wisely. Harlie

would likely be amenable to his company because he was part of the production team, and she'd want to suck up to him a bit. Victoria would have to play it loose and look for an opening.

It would suck rocks if Logan was the only one who could manage to get close to the woman. Just another opportunity for him to prove his worth and her to be lagging behind.

Although why she felt this competitive urge to best him, she had no idea—other than the fact she still resented how easily he'd managed to plant her on the workout mat too many times to count.

Growling, she turned on her side and tugged at the blanket again.

"Can't sleep?" Logan asked, his voice soft.

She opened her eyes and met his gaze. "Just thinking about how this week's gonna go."

"We'll figure it out. She's an actress. She likes attention. We'll give her some."

"You make that sound so easy. Everyone there, all twenty of her *closest friends*, will be vying for her attention."

"A person can't really have twenty close friends," he said and then grunted. "I can count mine on one hand."

"Same here." The four women of The Athena Project were it.

The overhead lights flickered on.

"That was quick," she muttered. So much for a nap.

"We have a driver. You can try to nap again on the trip out to the ranch."

She wrinkled her nose. "I think we need to use the time to go over our cover stories."

"And practice kissin', since we'll be roamin' around the estate after hours and can't be caught overtly checkin' out the security."

She laughed. "You really think we need to practice?"

"Nah. But mentionin' it makes you uncomfortable." His grin was wide and devilish.

She laughed again. "You're really enjoying this."

"I am."

Logan sighed and readjusted his seat, flipping off the blanket. She did the same, readying herself for landing. She was in a better mood now than she'd been in all day.

And why? Because he'd made her laugh? Because he'd kept her hot and off-balance ever since they'd been teamed up? Had he been playing her this entire time? She hadn't thought he was much more than the muscle of their team, but he'd just proven to her that he was smart, too. He'd pegged her from the start and had managed to get under her skin. He'd sparked her competitiveness, which had forced her to bring her A-game. Had he done it on purpose?

She ignored him as she folded her blanket and set it to the side. She'd have to keep on her toes to figure out a way to prove to him she was an equal partner. Otherwise, he'd leave this place thinking he'd had the harder job—babysitting *two* women.

CHAPTER 3

THEY ARRIVED at the ranch just before eleven p.m. to find the place lit up like the 4th of July, every porchlight gleaming, every window of the two-story luxury ranch house glowing.

"Looks like snoopin' around got a whole lot harder," Logan muttered under his breath.

They stopped on the circle drive in front of the porch. Men dressed in cowboy gear approached, offering to carry in their bags.

Their driver stepped out and opened the trunk. Logan tipped the driver and then turned back to the cowboys. "Not sure which room these need to go to…"

"Your name, sir?" one of the cowboys asked in an English accent.

"Logan Paxton," he said, providing the last name Sadie had given him.

The "cowboy" pulled out his iPhone and swiped his screen. "You're on the first floor, in the back. Your room opens onto the patio. Lucky you. Enjoy the party. Refreshments and drinks are being served beside the pool."

"Now, I get why Sadie said to wear our swimsuits under our clothes," Victoria said.

Logan drew a deep breath and offered her his elbow. "Shall we, dear?"

"We shall, darling," she said, with a wry twist of her lips. "It begins…"

They made their way up the steps and into a wide foyer lit by a chandelier made of intertwining elk antlers, through a large great room with several seating areas with sofas and chairs upholstered in leather and hides from exotic animals. The walls were decorated with Western art and trophy heads.

"Not the least ostentatious. Cozy, even," Victoria murmured sarcastically.

The sounds of laughter and many voices talking at once came through the French doors that opened onto a well-lit flagstone patio. Stepping outside, Logan noted the steam rising off the water. "Guess it's heated. I was wonderin'."

Victoria laughed. "Sadie told us that."

So, that had flown right past his head. Did she think he hadn't been paying any attention to what Sadie had said, or did she think he'd been too busy staring at the gorgeous movie star?

Victoria walked to one of the four Mexican chimineas set in the centers of seating areas to take the chill out of the night air for those taking advantage of the pool.

Logan glanced around, trying to spot their target, and found her, in the pool, standing topless amid a crowd of people; all were holding their fancy drinks in their hands while they bobbed in the water.

"Your four o'clock," he said, leaning toward Victoria.

"Gotcha. Guess we should introduce ourselves."

Logan grimaced. With the curious glances coming their way, he felt like they were on display. He gave Victoria a tight smile and strode toward a pair of empty loungers. There, he began stripping away his clothing.

A whistle sounded from the pool, and he glanced toward Harlie James. She had two fingers held between her lips. When their gazes met, she gave him a wave. "Come join us!"

He finished stripping, and then turned to Victoria. Instantly, he had to suck in a breath. Okay, so he'd known the woman's body was firm and well-muscled, but now, every lush curve was exposed. Her suit was meant to be a one-piece, he guessed, but most of the material was missing. Only a long triangular arrow of fabric attached the skimpy top to the tiny bottom in front. Desperate to hide his reaction, he moved toward the edge of the pool and jumped in. It was that or stand with his tongue hanging out and his "appreciation" growing inside his trunks.

When he glanced back her way, Victoria shook her head, her lips curving wryly, and strode with a sexy, side-to-side wag of her hips until she reached the pool where she surprised him by diving head-first into the water. When she surfaced, she was close to Harlie and her fan club.

Although the water was warmish, being submerged did the trick, and he swam toward the group, stopping beside Victoria, who was already introducing herself to the starlet.

"So nice to meet you," Harlie said, and then her gaze slid past her to Logan. Her eyes swept his shoulders and made their way downward. "You must be Sadie's guy. She said you were built like a brick house."

Logan grinned, careful not to let his gaze drop to her breasts, which were bobbing on the water. "I work out."

"I need to meet your personal trainer," Harlie teased.

Victoria raised her hand. "That would be me. I could give you some tips…"

Harlie dragged her gaze to Victoria. "That's great. I can use you on set."

"Maybe we could take some time here to talk about your goals," Victoria said.

Logan suppressed a chuckle as Victoria made her plug. She'd been looking for her "in", and it looked as though she'd found it.

They stayed a few minutes longer, meeting the rest of the group growing around the star, and then let the others push closer so they could surreptitiously edge away.

"Now might be a good time to scout out the house," Victoria said under her breath.

"I have the floorplan in my suitcase," Logan said. "We'll need to find Victoria's suite."

They had packed miniature cameras to install in the hallway leading to Harlie's room, and others to train on the windows from outside the house and out at the barn. With everyone's attention on their hostess, they left the pool and gathered up their clothing.

They were handed towels by staff as they neared the French doors and asked for directions to their room.

Once inside, they quickly shucked their towels and went to work, opening their cases to remove their gear.

Logan was careful to keep his gaze away from the large king-size bed.

"I'll just get changed," Victoria said then slipped into the bathroom.

Logan quickly pulled a dark, long-sleeve tee and dark-washed jeans from his bag and changed while she was out of the room. When she returned, he was ready after stuffing hardware into his pockets.

Standing side by side, they studied the floorplan of the house. Then Victoria folded it small enough to slide into the back pocket of her jeans.

"Where's that gift?" she asked.

Logan picked up the basket Sadie had had delivered to the plane, which was filled with high-end perfumes and chocolates—their excuse to seek out Harlie's suite—and they left their room.

They took their time walking through the house, keeping up a quiet conversation and giving each other smiles in case anyone was watching. They took the stairs to the second floor and spotted a middle-aged woman coming out of a bedroom. She went to a rolling cart and picked up a stack of white towels before turning and noticing them. "Do you need help finding your room?" she asked with a smile.

"No, we're lookin' for Ms. James's room," Logan said with a warm smile. He held up the basket. "We'd like to slip this inside. It's a gift to thank her for invitin' us to join her this weekend."

"I can take that for you," the woman said.

"I need to include a note," Victoria said, pulling a pen from her back pocket along with the folded floorplan sheet and holding them both up.

"Oh, well, follow me." The woman set the towels back onto the cart and led them down the hallway to the room at the end. Pulling out a ring of keys, she opened the door and stood to the side while Logan stepped into the room and glanced around. "Wow, this room is somethin' else," he said for the woman's benefit.

She gave him a wide smile. "It's the best room in this house. Mr. Porter, he's the owner of the place, uses this suite when he's here. He made it available to Ms. James."

Logan placed the basket on a desk in the sitting area. "Does Mr. Porter rent out this house very often?" he asked, giving Victoria cover as she planted a camera on the side of a light in the hallway behind where the woman stood.

"We're a dude ranch, but one that respects the privacy of our famous guests. So, he's very selective about who he allows to visit here."

"I understand," Logan said. "And I'm sure his guests are appreciative of his discretion." He glanced beyond her shoulder at Victoria. "Hon, do you have that note ready?"

The woman turned as Victoria clicked her pen closed and slid it back into her pocket. "Right here," she said cheerfully, holding the paper high and slipping past him. She pretended to slide the note into the basket then turned and wrapped her hands around his arm. "Ready to take that stroll under the stars?" she asked, smiling up at him.

"The sky's nice and clear for that," the woman said. "There's a gazebo near the river. If you head right from the front porch it's not far." She gave Logan a wink. "There's plenty of privacy there at night. I think everyone's out on the patio anyway."

Logan gave her a wide grin, which elicited a blush from the flustered woman. "Thank you…"

"Anita," she provided. "If you need anything…"

"I'll remember that…Anita."

Once they moved down the hall, Victoria gave his side a pinch. "Laying it on a little thick, weren't you?"

"We need allies," he drawled.

They retreated down the stairs and out the front door, waving at the cowboys who were seated on the steps, waiting for any stragglers who might still arrive.

They followed the path Anita had mentioned, not straying from it, because they didn't want anyone who might be watching to get curious about what they were doing. They found the gazebo, the roof shining brightly beneath the moon, its interior in shadows.

"I guess we should linger a bit," Victoria said.

"We can skirt the tree line going back so those cowboys don't see us. If we approach the house from the south, we can stay hidden while we install the cameras to cover the entrance and drive."

Victoria nodded. "We'll need another on the north side beneath her window."

"A couple in the barn area, and a couple on the patio—but we'll have to wait until everyone heads to bed for that."

Victoria wrinkled her nose. "Which could be the wee hours of the morning."

"We'll set an alarm. No use stayin' up all night."

Victoria leaned forward on a latticed rail and gazed out over the river. She took her phone from her back pocket and trained the flashlight over the water. "It's wider than I thought it'd be."

"They flyfish here. Need a river, not a stream."

"You flyfish?" she asked, giving him a sideways glance.

"Naw. I don't like wadin' into the river up to my ass. I prefer sittin' on the bank, a cooler of beer beside me, while my line bobs on the surface."

"Huh."

"What?"

"I just can't picture you being that lazy."

He laughed. "A lazy day is a reward for hard work where I come from. Do you fish?"

"Not ever." She grimaced and gave an exaggerated shiver. "I can't imagine putting wiggly worms or little fish on hooks."

"Ya know, you can catch fish with artificial flies."

"I know. Still, having to sit for hours, having to be *quiet*..."

He chuckled. "You've done surveillance. I know you've been still and quiet for long periods of time."

"But doing that *on purpose*...for pleasure."

He grinned in the darkness. "So, what do you like to do *on purpose* for pleasure?"

She shrugged. "I...like working out."

"I mean, for *fun*?"

"Well, I like movies."

"Ah. So, you *can* enjoy sittin' still..."

"I don't exactly sit still." She grinned sheepishly, her teeth flashing in the shadows. "I tend to drive anyone sitting near me crazy."

He groaned. "Oh, so you're one of those."

She reached out and pushed his shoulder. "What do you mean by that?"

"Runnin' commentary. Catchin' errors." When she didn't deny it, he added, "Do you have a hard time suspendin' disbelief?"

Again, she shrugged. "I guess."

"I take it superhero movies aren't high on your list of movies to watch."

She shrugged. "I...kind of like the Thor movies."

He nodded. "So, you like beefcake and humor."

"If a movie's going to be that ridiculous, it should make you laugh."

"What about action? Did you like *Die Hard*?"

"I prefer something a little more realistic."

"So, action, but realistic. Vin Diesel's out."

"And the Rock. Did you see *San Andreas*?"

He laughed. "I couldn't get past the trailer."

"Maybe we should stick to documentaries…"

"Our date nights would be pretty borin'."

She turned around and leaned her elbows on the railing. "You do date nights?"

He hadn't since high school, but he didn't think it was exactly kosher to admit his current version of date night usually ended in bed. "Not really."

She nodded, and her eyes narrowed. "So, you only do hook-ups, don't you?"

He cleared his throat. "Um, maybe we should head back and see about getting those cameras installed."

"I'm right!" she said, crowing.

He was glad of the darkness. His cheeks were on fire. "I haven't spent enough time in one place in years to do…relationships."

She sighed. "I hear you."

Something snapped nearby, and they both straightened. And because this was part of the plan, albeit a half-joking one, he reached for her forearm, dragged her up against his body, and kissed her.

CHAPTER 4

ALTHOUGH THEY HADN'T PRACTICED, their noses aligned perfectly.

That was Victoria's first bemused thought. The second was that his lips were oddly soft and firm… and warm. For a moment, she stood suspended in the moment, discovering his kiss. When he didn't move to deepen it, she blinked open her eyes and realized he was looking to the side.

Instantly, she shook off the wonder and paid attention. Was there someone out there? Or had it been some random animal crunching on a twig?

Another snap and soft pads sounded. Definitely bipedal. Someone was out there.

She slipped a hand between their bodies and tapped his shoulder.

"Do you see anything?" she whispered when he lifted his lips.

He made a soft grunting sound and shook his head.

"Do we wait them out?"

A hand slid around her and settled on the small of her back. "You always this impatient?" he asked, a hint of humor in his voice.

Seeing as their torsos were plastered together, she could hardly just stand there. Not when she was so tempted to lean into his body. She wrinkled her nose.

He must have seen that grimace and bent again, resting his mouth on hers. Not pressing, just touching. And she found this non-kiss extremely maddening.

"We can't just stand here forever," she said, her words muffled against his lips.

"What do you suggest?"

His voice had deepened. Her body responded with a shiver traveling up her spine.

When he shifted his stance and one leg crept between hers, she almost yelped, but that hand on her back kept her still as he applied pressure between her legs.

Wordless now, her heart revved, pounding in her ears. She couldn't look left or right; she also didn't want to press against his shoulders to put some space between them. Her breasts were tightening, the tips of her nipples scraping against the thin lace cups of her bra.

Logically, she knew he was just trying to get her to be quiet, but now…and yeah…she wasn't in the mood to talk, but she sure wanted to moan.

At last, he eased his thigh away and gently held her hips while he took a step back. "They're headin' toward the house. Must've seen us in the gazebo."

She cleared her throat and pushed back her hair, thankful for the shadows which hid her fiery cheeks. "I think there was only one individual."

"Seems odd for someone to head this way without a partner," he said, his voice sounding slightly raspy.

"Maybe it was one of the cowboys, just checking to see where we'd gone…?"

"Maybe, but the first time I heard a sound it was comin' from the direction of the river."

"So, maybe someone doing what we're supposed to be doing—checking this place out?" At his nod, she frowned. "Well, we still have to set up those cameras and then try to get some sleep." Although how much sleep she'd get lying next to him was a huge question now. She couldn't forget the sensation of his thick, muscled thigh sliding between hers…

"Yeah, let's skirt the tree line until we get to Harlie's side of the house. We'll work our way around the back behind the fence surroundin' the patio."

"Gotcha," she said, forcing her thoughts back to

the tasks at hand as he obviously had. They had a job to do. And four more days to get through pretending they were a couple. An intimate couple. Why did it feel like that wasn't going to be the hard part of this assignment?

AFTER THEY'D INSTALLED cameras beneath Harlie's window, out at the barn/parking area, and then moved around to the other side of the house to do the same in the shadows beyond the porch, they skirted the house the same way they'd come, arriving back on the trail that led to the gazebo. Logan stood with Victoria, looking across at the cowboys, who were sitting on the steps, leaning back lazily on their elbows.

Logan and Victoria were still outside the halo of light from the porch's lamps. He drew them both to a halt then turned to face her. "We need to look like we've been makin' out." He didn't give her any more warning than that before thrusting his hands in her hair and messing it up a bit. Then he bent and kissed her hard, rubbing his lips against hers to plump them up.

She didn't freeze like she had the last time and even tilted her head back a little to let him deepen the kiss. Cupping her cheeks, he decided it wouldn't hurt to do a little exploring. Just for practice. *Right.*

When he licked along the seam of her lips, she slowly opened to him. Her fingers slid up to cup his face then framed his ears while her fingertips dug into his scalp.

Nice. She tasted nice. The tip of her tongue met his and slid tentatively, at first, and then more deeply.

A rumble rose up inside him, and her mouth curved beneath his. When he lifted his head, she was grinning. He guessed turnabout was fair play. When he'd slipped his thigh between hers back at the gazebo, he'd done it to distract her because she'd been talking too much. Now, he was the one a little breathless, thoughts scattered to the wind.

Jesus, this woman's mouth was made for sin, and he couldn't help but think of all the ways he'd love to use it to pave his way to Hell.

"Think that did it," she said, reaching up to rub her thumb over his lower lip. Then she stepped around him and walked toward the porch, her backside wagging.

Damn if he wasn't the happy puppy following her.

They passed the cowboys who didn't bother rising as they approached. One of them tipped his hat to Logan in a little manly salute of appreciation for his woman. He returned it with a glare. He was only *acting* jealous. *Uh-huh.*

Once inside, they headed toward the French

doors leading to the patio. There were still a few people in the pool. Harlie had moved to a seating area, having wrapped a fluffy towel around her torso while she combed her fingers through her wet hair. Hangers-on sat in the loungers beside hers; all of them had drinks in their hands or sitting on small tables next to the loungers.

"They're going to be there a while," Victoria said. Then she yawned.

"We should head back to the room. You can catch that nap you never got while I check the feeds from the cameras we already installed. I can wake you when the patio goes dark so we can install the last cameras."

Her gaze stayed glued on the patio, but she gave a little nod. "Sounds good."

It probably sounded good because he'd just told her he wouldn't be joining her in bed right away. They both needed a little space to cool off.

He wondered if she'd admit it, if only to herself, that something had happened between them when they'd been "pretending" to kiss.

Grasping her hand, because he didn't want her forgetting too quickly just how hot things had gotten, he pulled her behind him as they headed back through the house to their room.

Once inside, he quickly dropped her hand, and without glancing back, headed toward his laptop which he'd already set on the desk. Behind him, he heard a huffed breath and smiled. The sounds of zippers scratching and footsteps padding away, followed by the closing of the bathroom door, allowed him a moment to release a deep breath.

He'd thought the hard part of being her partner for this mission would be keeping her safe. He'd never considered he'd have to fight himself to keep his hands off her. However, one kiss and one glide of his thigh between hers had been enough to ratchet up the complications.

Sure, he'd recognized from the start that she was a beautiful woman, but he'd been able to set that aside because he'd never go there. Not when they had to work closely together. Plus, it looked like Jake intended for them to be field partners for the foreseeable future. Again, the old shitting in your own backyard adage came to mind but was equally as off-putting as it had been the first time. If they went *there*, and things didn't work out, how could they get past it?

This job was important to them both. He'd left the SEALs, ready to find work just a little less dangerous, where he didn't have to worry as much about teammates dying around him. He'd seen too much death. Still, he was an admitted adrenaline junkie, so he'd known he'd be looking for security work of some kind. This Protectors gig was a good fit. Now, he couldn't screw it up by screwing around with his partner.

Yes, he'd noticed that several of the Protectors in the Colorado office had hooked up with the women they'd guarded. Roman McClain had hooked up with his Athena Project partner, Beck, and that seemed to work for them, but Logan had never been particularly…monogamous. He didn't know how to "do" couples. He liked women, had enjoyed friendships in the past that had included some pretty sexy benefits, but this was different. He and Victoria had to see each other, day in and day out. There'd be no escape when things fizzled between them.

Someone could get hurt. Not him. Because he wasn't made that way. He liked casual, no entanglements. Nothing…sticky. Or too emotional.

He powered up the laptop and hit the icon on the screen that opened up all the camera views in little boxes. There was no activity except for on the patio. A woman was dancing. Harlie had donned a tank top that clung to her braless breasts, and she threw back her head and headed toward the woman, coming up behind her to hold her hips. Soon, they faced each other, egged on by their audience as they swayed and bounced to the music.

Harlie was the kind of woman he tended to gravitate toward when he was looking for company. Someone who lived in the moment, ready for a good time.

Victoria was…

Logan frowned, unable to continue the thought because he realized there was a lot he didn't know about his partner. Sure, she was a pain in the ass. Snarky. Combative. Sure of herself.

That confidence was sexy as hell. He remembered the glint in her eye when she'd sashayed past him and the cowboys on the porch.

No. That confidence could get her killed. She thought she was tougher than she was. He had eighty pounds on her, and still, she'd been unwilling to concede she couldn't beat him in hand-to-hand. The woman didn't know when to quit.

Back to the puzzle that was Victoria. He knew she and Beck went way back. That she'd recently left the FBI, but he didn't know why. The women who'd joined the Athena Project were all very capable, all from different alphabet agencies of the government. They brought different perspectives, connections, and skills to the Project.

The bathroom door opened, and steam and perfume filled the air. He glanced behind him and saw Victoria bent over her suitcase, sifting through the contents. She wore a small pair of gym shorts and a tank. Damn, she was all legs, pink and curvy. Her rounded bottom stretched her shorts in a way that caused his balls to cramp.

When she shot him a quick glance, he couldn't pretend his glance had been casual.

Her eyebrows drew into a fierce frown. "You see who's dancing with Harlie?"

He blinked and glanced back at the screen. Then he clicked on the box of the feed that gave him the best view, and it filled the screen. "Isn't that Adnan Khan?"

Victoria came closer and bent toward the screen. "Thought she was scared he'd tried to kidnap her in Costa Rica."

From the way the pair was dancing, so close there was no light between their bodies, Harlie had apparently thrown aside her caution.

Logan noted the man was wearing a suit, and his tie was loosened. He topped Harlie's five-foot-nine by maybe three inches. His beard was short, his features hawkish. His expression as he watched Harlie with his dark, piercing gaze was…intent and possessive.

Harlie's earlier exuberance, which had lavished everyone around her with warmth and fun, was more subdued now. Her gaze was locked on Adnan.

"She doesn't look afraid," Victoria murmured.

No, but all her attention was on Adnan, to the exclusion of everyone else around her. He noted the glum expressions of some of her entourage, including the worried frown coming from her personal assistant.

"What's the assistant's name?" he asked.

"Elaine…Spivey," Victoria murmured. "She

doesn't look very happy. And those two…" she said, tapping the screen, "if looks could kill."

He glanced at the couple who'd shared the lounger next to Harlie's. Both their mouths were pinched, and their eyes glared daggers at Adnan. "Their pictures weren't in the dossier."

"We have a copy of the lodge's guest list. We can go through it…process of elimination."

"I can go through it," he said in a tight voice. "You need rest."

She glanced sideways at him then looked downward. Maybe she'd finally noticed that her hand rested on his shoulder, and her knee pressed against his thigh. It couldn't be she'd noticed that his jeans were a little tight in front.

Logan breathed shallowly to keep from inhaling more of her floral scent. He was already too aware of her warm, steamy skin.

"You'll wake me?" she asked, not moving away. Her mouth, which he had tasted an hour ago, was parted. Inviting.

This was fucking torture. "Yeah," he bit out. "I'll wake you."

Her mouth curved, and she bent toward him.

His breath held, waiting for her lips to touch his, but at the last moment, she turned her head and kissed his cheek. "Night."

When she moved away, he heard a soft snicker.

Logan eased apart his legs under the desk and

leaned back in his chair. But he wasn't angry because she'd teased him. No, he was grinning.

Two could play this game.

All his earlier thoughts about backyards and partners being off-limits were deep-sixed in his mind. While he placed names to faces and whittled down the list of who was who, he never lost track of the woman lying in the king-size bed just feet away.

For the first time, he didn't resent this cake-walk of a security detail. Beck and Jake expected them to learn to function as a team over the next few days, but he thought, maybe, they'd also seen something he and Victoria hadn't. Their attraction wasn't something they should ignore. And it wasn't a "problem" necessarily, just something they had to address, head-on.

Or hands-on.

Definitely, hands-on.

CHAPTER 5

Victoria sat in a chair at a ridiculously long table in the ranch house kitchen. Eight early birds were seated there, including herself and Logan.

How he managed to look so rested and chipper was a mystery to her. The only sleep he'd gotten had been after four that morning. When the patio had finally cleared and the lights went out, they'd gotten their chance to install the last surveillance cameras.

After they'd finished, she hadn't given him a second thought as she'd crawled beneath the sheets and fallen asleep in an instant; she'd been that tired.

Waking up next to him hadn't been as...*thought-less*...an experience.

An alarm—*his*—had beeped, jarring her from some pleasant dream. His arms had tightened around her, and her eyes had popped open instantly.

His body had been spooned close against her back.

When had that happened?

She'd held her breath, wondering if he was awake, and then thinking maybe she should pretend to sleep until he turned off his alarm, which would call for him to unwind his arms from around her. Maybe it had been a cowardly choice, but she hadn't been ready to face a conversation about this. So, she'd drawn a deep breath and let it out slowly, making a little snoring sound to add a little realism.

His chest had shaken against her back. Then his quiet chuckles had stirred the hair on the side of her cheek. "Really?" he'd drawled before sputtering into laughter again.

She'd cleared her throat. "I think that's your alarm," she said, determined to ignore the issue.

He'd slowly dragged his arms from over and under her, likely *purposely* letting his hands slide a little slower as he'd cupped her sides. Then he'd scooted away his hips, but not before she'd felt the sizable erection he'd sported. It had been impossible to miss, rubbing against her backside.

Not until he'd left the bed and headed to the bathroom had she flung out her arms and rested on her back, pulling in deep breaths of air because, holy shit, that had been awkward as hell.

But the question that had taunted her was who had spooned whom? Had she snuggled into him? Had he gathered her close?

Worse, had she felt him up as they'd slept? Her dream, right before that damn alarm had gone off, had been pretty graphic…

Those were all questions she wasn't sure she wanted to be answered.

"Pass the potatoes?"

Logan's deep voice pulled her from her reverie. She reached for the large bowl of hash browns, gave herself a reasonably-sized portion, then watched him cover half his plate with two heaping ladles full of the crispy, fried potatoes.

When the bacon came, she added two slices to her plate, then thought she'd better take what she wanted now because there would be nothing left when he was done. She used the tongs to add two more slices, and then gave him a pointed stare when she passed the platter.

Eggs were served in two dishes. One with scrambled eggs "smothered and covered" with onions and cheese, the other served plain. She chose the onions to discourage any "pretend" kissing because she didn't know if she could handle it this morning.

Anita, the older woman they'd met the evening before, roamed around the table filling coffee cups. Victoria wished she had a larger mug as she turned her cup in its saucer to signal she needed hers filled.

Anita filled Victoria's cup and then moved on to Logan.

Logan gave her a warm smile, which had the woman instantly blushing. His "thank you" was also a little too friendly from Victoria's point of view.

When Anita moved on, Logan arched an eyebrow. "What?"

Victoria didn't answer but plucked a biscuit from the basket circulating the table and plopped it on her plate.

Logan took three.

Victoria stared at those three hot biscuits thinking they represented all that was wrong with her world. How unfair was it that he could have three when she had to work out extra hard to make sure her one biscuit didn't add an inch to her ass? And he'd probably smother it in butter and honey, which she had to avoid, although buttered and honeyed biscuits smelled like manna from heaven this morning.

He held out the jar of honey he'd just closed. "You want some?"

"No."

"You were staring at it."

She swallowed because her mouth had filled with saliva. "Was not."

He shook his head and closed the biscuit he'd split before he'd slathered it with butter and drowned it in honey. His groan as he took a bite sounded almost sexual. Or how she imagined he'd sound during sex.

She finished her breakfast in a worse mood than when she'd begun it.

They didn't linger over their meal, instead heading out to the porch to sit on a cushioned loveseat as they drank more coffee while she checked her tablet to see what was happening inside the house. "Did you see what time Harlie headed back to her room last night?" she asked after glancing around to make sure no one else was nearby.

"It was after three," he said softly. "And she wasn't alone."

"Adnan?"

He nodded.

"Well, that's interesting. Did Trevor Hanson ever make it in?" she asked. The male lead actor of the movie had accepted Harlie's weekend invitation but hadn't been at the party the previous night.

"Nope." He stretched and reached out his arm to place it over her shoulder as the front door opened and the couple who'd shown disapproval of the Adnan-Harlie hookup the night before stepped outside.

Logan offered them a smile and waved at the carafe of coffee on the table in front of their seat. "Join us?"

The couple offered polite smiles and settled in chairs opposite them.

"I'm Logan Tackett," Logan said, "and this is my fiancée, Victoria Bunting."

Victoria managed to contain her grimace at the last name Sadie had assigned her.

"Cal Gross, and this is my wife, Pauline."

"We haven't met," Logan continued. "I'm with the production company for the film."

Cal's eyes brightened. "That's great. We can't wait to get to work."

"And what do you do?"

Cal blinked. "I'm the lead cinematographer. Pauline does makeup."

Cal acted as though they should've recognized his name.

Victoria eyed Pauline and wondered why the woman hadn't worked on her own face. Her undereye circles were as dark as hers had been before she'd used concealer to hide her lack of sleep.

"I've already been out to the site," Cal said.

"Spent a couple of weeks scouting locations with the director."

Logan smiled and nodded. "Heard there've already been some problems."

Cal nodded. "They've been building sets. A roof caved in on a honkytonk set. We laid tracks for the cameras for an action scene, but somehow, the rails shifted right before we rehearsed a long action sequence. We lost an entire rig and a pricey Nikon when they flew off the rail."

"Then there was the fiasco with the caterers," Pauline said. "We had locals providing food to the setup crew, and three ended up in the hospital due to food poisoning."

"Surprised you didn't hear about that," Cal said. "They had to scout a new caterer and get them contracted quickly so they'll be ready to roll once everyone arrives on set."

"I'm brand new to the team," Logan murmured. "Sadie brought me on at the last minute."

"Have you worked on anything I'd know about?"

"Nah. I've been out of the country working on another future project for Sadie."

Victoria decided the conversation needed a bit of redirect before they ran out of believable responses. "So, have you worked on a Sadie McClain film before?" she asked the couple.

"First time I've had the privilege," Cal said. "I worked on Harlie's last project though."

"Me, too," Pauline said. "She's a sweetheart to work with. I was in charge of hair and makeup—exclusively, for her."

Victoria leaned forward and bit her lip like she was hesitant to ask. "The man who showed up last night...the one she was dancing with... They seemed to really hit it off."

Pauline blew out a deep breath. "I shouldn't say..."

But Victoria knew she would. The woman's mouth formed the same pinched line as it had the previous night. She was bristling with disapproval.

Pauline leaned toward Victoria and whispered, "That was Adnan. Her former boyfriend."

"Didn't look so former," Victoria whispered back.

"They had a bit of a falling out." She sniffed. "I hear everything. People talk to their stylists, you know. And she was a wreck on the last set. Broke it off with him. He was too controlling. Wanted her to quit acting. Can you imagine that? She's going to be a big star."

Victoria shook her head and widened her eyes. "Do you think he's trying to get back with her?"

Pauline shook her head. "The way she looked when he came out on the patio—I think she was shocked. But he turned that stare of his on her, and she just…"

"Melted?" Victoria whispered. She'd felt that way a time or two in her life.

Pauline rolled her eyes. "She's not thinking. Harlie's…a free spirit. He's not going to change that."

Cal cleared his throat. "We really shouldn't gossip, dear."

Pauline blinked and leaned back.

Knowing there wouldn't be any further intel to squeeze from Pauline until she could catch her alone, Victoria glanced at Logan. "Have you looked at the list of activities the ranch has planned for guests today?"

"I saw something about an ATV trek into the mountains."

"That sounds like fun." She glanced back at the couple across from them. "Will you be going?"

Pauline grimaced. "I'm not good with speed. Be warned. Harlie drives like a bat out of hell."

She laughed. "I think I can keep up. What about you, Cal?"

He shook his head. "I've got a Zoom call with the director today. I'll pass."

Logan and Victoria stood.

"It was nice talking with you," Logan said, reaching out to shake Cal's hand. "I'm sure we'll have plenty more opportunities to get to know you."

Victoria lifted her hand and curled her fingers in goodbye then headed back inside the ranch house.

"Check the dining room?" Logan asked.

"No need," Victoria said, glancing at her tablet. "Harlie's already out at the barn. With Adnan. And they have a little entourage."

"We can cut through the patio to get there quicker."

She was glad they were already dressed in their Western gear—jeans, long-sleeve pearl-button shirts, and boots. Whether Harlie was looking to ride a horse or an ATV, they were ready.

"I'll run to our room to grab our hats."

Once she'd retrieved them and deposited the tablet on the bed, they found the group gathered at the side of the barn. Harlie was holding onto Adnan's arm, and he looked...besotted. His gaze barely left her face as Harlie's friends chattered around her.

And who could blame him? The blonde wore the same Western gear as the rest of them, but her clothing was better fitted—or perhaps her curves were better defined. She had a perfect hourglass figure with a narrow waist that emphasized the lush curves above and below. Victoria felt a moment's envy but reassured herself with the thought Harlie's conditioning and frame couldn't be pressed to do the things she could.

Besides, all those extra curves just got in the way of things.

Yeah, she wasn't the least bit envious. She huffed a laugh at herself. Harlie was as naturally gifted as Sadie in the beauty department.

Her gaze slid to Logan who didn't seem as impressed with their hostess's figure. His gaze was checking out the people gathered around her and seemed to snag on Harlie's assistant, Elaine, whose lips were crimped into a narrow line.

Harlie's head swung their way, and she gave them a bright smile and waved them over. "Join us! We're about to head out on the trails."

Logan smiled. "On horseback?"

Harlie laughed. "Horses leave me sore in all the wrong places."

Chuckles sounded all around her.

Adnan's mouth seemed to tense in disapproval.

An interesting dynamic. Harlie seemed unaware her boyfriend didn't appear happy with her word choice.

"The foreman, Emmet, is getting the guys to bring the ATVs around," Harlie said. "I'll tell him to get one more ready to go. You've driven one before, right? You'll have to keep up."

Logan grinned and nodded. He slung an arm

around Victoria's shoulders. "She's not very experienced."

"That's okay," Harlie said, winking at her. "All you have to do is hold onto him. I'm sure he won't mind."

Smiling, Victoria reached around Logan and gave him a side hug—followed by a hard pinch that had him wincing—and then chuckling.

He'd made sure he was the one in the driver's seat again.

CHAPTER 6

THE TRAILS around the ranch wound up into steeper hills. The ranch sat in the Jackson Hole Valley, surrounded by the Teton Mountain and Gros Ventre ranges. Soon after leaving on a gravel trail through a pasture, they followed an even narrower dirt track that had them riding through trees and increasingly rocky terrain.

Logan smiled to himself as they motored along, keeping far enough back from the rider in front of them so that he and Victoria weren't eating the dust the four-wheeler stirred up. Maybe it hadn't been the most gentlemanly thing he'd done, excluding her from driving the ATV, but he enjoyed seeing her cheeks blush and her eyes narrow when he managed to gain an advantage. It gave him a perverse delight. And it aroused him.

Hell, everything about the woman aroused him.

Which was why he revved the gas every now and then, jerking them forward so that she had to keep her arms wound tightly around his middle or risk being dumped off. He liked having her hands on him.

They left the gravel trail and headed cross-country, climbing hills and sliding in loose shale. The riders ahead of him whooped with delight.

In the lead, Harlie was having a grand old time, her hand lifting every now and then to raise a fist in the air. Behind her, Adnan leaned forward on his vehicle. When they rounded a curve, Logan noted the man's expression. His lips were turned downward, and his brow was lowered in a fierce frown.

Logan didn't get what the man saw in Harlie, seeing as he disapproved of everything she did. He'd known men like him before. They thought they could change their partner, and if they managed to pull back on the lead, their partner was never happy. He'd be better off finding someone who wanted to be cossetted and set upon a pedestal.

He'd have to keep a close eye on the guy to make sure he left Harlie the option of dumping his ass.

Or at least he'd keep an eye on him for as long as this gig lasted. Maybe he should have a conversation with the woman, or discuss it with Victoria, so she could warn Harlie that Adnan just wasn't right for her. And that he might be dangerous.

What little had been conveyed about the man in the documents Swede, Hank's tech and intel guy, had put together didn't paint a pretty picture.

Adnan had ties to the current Saudi leader, a man known for his barbarity. Definitely not someone who accepted international laws or any ethical rules of behavior.

They reached the top of a ridgeline, and Harlie followed it. Below them, the ranch was completely out of sight with glimpses here and there of the Gros Ventre River in the distance. The view was majestic and as far from anything he'd ever experienced being raised in Oklahoma or from his many tours in the sandbox. No, they didn't have mountains like this. And the mountain ranges in Afghanistan hadn't been this beautiful—surrounded by green hills that suddenly jutted upwards into soaring peaks.

Harlie slowed and turned off her engine. The rest of her followers pulled in beside her. She reached into a saddlebag on the back of her ATV and brought out a bottle and paper cups.

Behind him, Victoria climbed off then reached over and gave his shoulder a thump. "That's for jerking me around, asshole," she muttered. But her lips curved at the corners before she walked away with an exaggerated wag of her rear.

He grinned and climbed off, heading toward the group now filling their cups with wine.

"Isn't this fantastic?" Harlie said, sweeping out her arms as though to encompass the view. She walked to the edge of a drop-off and leaned over it, glancing downward. "Wow, I didn't realize we were so high up."

Adnan walked close to her and reached for her wrist. "The rock is shale. I wouldn't stand so close to the edge because it could easily break off."

She glanced over her shoulder at him. "Always a buzzkill," she said, but her tone was affectionate.

Adnan shook his head then drew a deep breath. "Shall we head back?"

Logan checked his watch. It was already nearing noon, and his stomach was rumbling.

"I wouldn't mind heading back to grab a bite to eat," Harlie said. She glanced around the group. "You ready to head back?"

Everyone was in agreement, smiling as they walked back to their ATVs.

Once again, Harlie led the procession back down the steep trail, Adnan following close behind. This time, Logan followed Adnan, not wanting too much distance between his and Harlie's vehicle.

About halfway down, he frowned because they were traveling a little too fast for the conditions. They skirted a large rock wall then Harlie zigged left and glanced over her shoulder. Her eyes were wide.

Something was wrong.

Logan shouted over his shoulder at Victoria, "Hold on! Harlie's in trouble." Then he took his finger off the gas, clicked his foot on the gear shift, pushed the gas again, and the ATV shot forward.

He passed Adnan then pulled in beside Harlie. "What's wrong?" he shouted.

She didn't glance his way, but he could see that her left hand was squeezing the brake all the way to the handlebar. "The brakes aren't working!" she shouted back.

"Gear down!"

She nodded, and her ATV bucked, the engine whirring loudly as she shifted the gear.

They reached a split in the trail, one heading downward, the other up. He lifted his hand to point her toward the one heading higher.

She shook her head, clearly panicking, her face white and her lips tightening against her teeth.

"Do it, Harlie!" he said, then fell slightly behind her so she could make the sharp turn.

She closed her eyes briefly, as though in prayer, and then made the turn. As it climbed, her ATV began to slow.

Logan came up beside her again. "Just ride it out. Don't give it any gas."

The ATV slowed, crawling as they reached a low peak.

Logan held his breath, getting ready to tell her to jump, but her ATV finally slowed and stopped, sputtering out.

As soon as it did, Harlie leaped off the four-wheeler and stood bent over with her hands on her knees as she dragged in deep breaths.

Adnan came to a stop behind them, cut his engine, climbed off, and ran to Harlie. "Are you all right?"

She nodded but reached out to clutch his arm. Logan and Victoria climbed off, and Logan headed straight to Harlie's ATV. Going to a knee, he inspected the front wheels and saw a dark, wet stain.

"Brake fluid?" Victoria asked softly, leaning over him.

"Yeah. And the line's been punctured."

They shared a glance.

Logan pushed upward and returned to Harlie. "There's no fixing your ATV here. You'll have to ride with someone else back to the ranch. We'll let the staff there know where they can find their vehicle."

Harlie's gaze went to Adnan, whose expression was dark.

"You will ride with me," he said.

Logan wasn't pleased when she nodded, but if

Adnan was responsible, he likely wouldn't sabotage his own ride.

"Maybe we should keep the trip back under the speed of light," Victoria said, waggling her eyebrows, which made Harlie laugh.

The trip back was more somber. Everyone looked relieved to arrive safely back at the barn. Logan met with the hands to let them know there'd been a problem on the mountain and approximately where to find the damaged vehicle, but he didn't mention the puncture mark he'd discovered. That was something he'd let Jake back at the Brotherhood Protectors know about.

Apparently, the incidents on the set weren't confined to the set. He glanced around the group who'd accompanied Harlie this morning, but other than Adnan, no one stood out. Then again, when would Adnan have had a chance to puncture her line?

He remembered the foreman named Emmet, who'd driven Harlie's vehicle right up to her. He'd have a conversation with the man and try to figure out if her riding that particular ATV had been a random happenstance.

Somehow, he didn't think so.

Victoria followed Harlie inside while Logan lingered at the barn. She was sure he was likely in investigation mode to see if he could figure out who was responsible for the puncture in the brake line.

Her job now was to stick closely to their client, who didn't know she was one.

Luckily, Harlie headed straight to the kitchen with her entourage trailing behind her.

Victoria took a seat at the long table, not close enough to draw undue attention, but keeping both Harlie and Adnan in her line of sight.

Staff approached the table. Drinks were soon served. Harlie requested a Bellini, which led to most of her crew ordering the same drink. Victoria ordered a soda, as did Adnan.

Soon, platters of food arrived at the table. A large Mexican casserole and taco ingredients were passed around.

Victoria served herself then glanced sideways when Logan slid in beside her and reached for the platter of crispy taco shells she'd been about to hand off to the next diner.

She'd selected two taco shells. He piled his plate with five. When the casserole made it to them, she placed a small, tidy square next to her tacos, and he carved out an entire row to place on his plate.

Quickly, she reached out a finger to pick up one corner of his row, which was overhanging his plate. She shoved it back onto the rim.

Logan grabbed her finger and brought it to his

mouth, where he sucked it clean—and then winked at her.

Heat filled her face, and she glanced away, her gaze colliding with Harlie, who was grinning. The actress gave Victoria a thumbs up.

They filled their tacos and began eating.

In between bites of mostly salad-filled taco, she leaned toward Logan. "What did you find out?"

"That the newest ATV was assigned to the person who paid for this weekend."

She frowned. "Then, anyone who might have guessed that would happen…"

"Yeah. I told Emmet that Harlie's four-wheeler lost brake fluid. He didn't blink. He seemed genuinely perplexed that a brand-new ATV'd had that problem."

"So, someone who knew the ranch's habit of assigning the newest vehicle decided to put Harlie at risk…?"

"Or someone accepted a bribe to make it happen."

Which seemed more likely, now that they knew about the problems on the set.

"On paper, Adnan makes sense," Logan said.

"But you saw how concerned he was," she murmured.

Logan sighed. "Yeah. I don't think he would want any physical harm to come her way."

"He just wants her to give up her career and

choose a life with him." Victoria took another bite. She couldn't imagine someone like Harlie, who'd worked her tail off to be where she was, giving up everything for a man.

"Too bad we can't tell Harlie why we're here," he murmured.

"Might not be able to keep it a secret for long. We can't have eyes on her when she's behind closed doors. The big question is whether this is about Harlie or about the movie. She might just be a target of opportunity since work on the set has slowed for the time being so folks get a break before hitting it hard next week."

More people started filtering into the dining room, taking seats, all jockeying to be as close as they could get to Harlie who had positioned herself at the center of the table.

A very handsome man entered the dining room, catching Victoria's eye. "Our leading man has arrived," she murmured.

With dark auburn hair, a leanly muscled frame, and eyes that looked a little otherworldly they were such a deep green, he walked with confidence into the room, pulling every glance.

Trevor Hanson was definitely easy on the eyes.

"Trevor!" Harlie exclaimed and popped up from her seat, running around it to fling herself against the man's chest.

Trevor laughed and gave her a hug before gripping her upper arms and holding her away. "Aren't you a sight for sore eyes?"

Harlie blushed. "Have you eaten? Care to join us?"

He glanced around the table. All the seats near Harlie were filled. His gaze went to the empty chair beside Victoria, and she bit back a groan. The last thing she wanted to do was make idle chatter with an actor.

When Harlie headed back around the table to her seat, and Trevor sat next to Victoria, Logan growled a little under his breath.

Victoria shot him a glance.

One side of his mouth was lifted with a hint of a smirk.

She gave him an elbow to his ribs, and Logan grunted then rubbed his side. Then he reached his hand across Victoria, extending it to Trevor. "We haven't met. I'm Logan Tackett, part of Sadie's production team. This is my fiancée, Victoria Bunting."

Victoria jumped at the word "fiancée."

"Trevor Hanson." His gaze dropped to Victoria. "Are you an actress?"

She laughed. "Not hardly. I'm a personal trainer."

Trevor shook his head. "You're certainly pretty enough to be an actress."

She dropped her chin and pretended to be

pleased with his compliment. "Well, thank you." Time to *act*. "This week is *soooo* exciting. I can't believe I'm here with Harlie James and Trevor Hanson," she said with just enough enthusiasm he might worry about her fangirling all over him. Now, he'd give her a wide berth anytime she was near. Which would keep her free to follow Harlie around.

Trevor patted her hand lying on the table. "We're all just people, Victoria. You don't have to treat us any differently than you would any other friend." And he said *friend* with a little extra emphasis while giving her a sly wink.

Victoria stiffened and forced a smile. Okay, so she'd misjudged him. He liked adulation. Maybe he also thought an engaged woman was a bit of a challenge. Dammit.

CHAPTER 7

Logan dove beneath the water and swam the length of the pool, turned, and completed another lap. Not many were in the water just yet, seeing as Harlie was still holding court from her lounger.

The patio was alight with tiki torches, and buffet tables had been set out in one corner of the patio. Prime rib was being sliced and served, along with foil-wrapped baked potatoes, trays of cooked vegetables, and salad items with every garnish imaginable.

Trevor sat in the seat next to Harlie's, sharing the attention of her hangers-on with poor Adnan sitting across from her, his gaze dark and his mouth turned down at the corners.

Logan had left Victoria to keep an eye on Harlie while he'd taken advantage of the empty pool. He hadn't gotten in a workout today, and his body felt it. After several laps, he felt more relaxed and hauled himself over the edge of the pool.

His gaze went to Victoria, who quickly blinked and turned her head toward Harlie.

Logan grinned, knowing she'd been checking him out. Just like he had since the moment she'd exited the bathroom wearing a white bikini, a silky covering tied around her waist, and crystal-studded sandals. Good Lord, even Trevor had done a double-take when she'd stepped out onto the patio, but Harlie had quickly pulled his attention back, discarding her coverup and sitting in the tiniest red bikini Logan had ever seen. It wasn't anything more than three small triangles held in place by skinny straps. The woman may as well have been naked, and her *former* boyfriend wasn't one bit happy about that fact.

He might also be looking sulky since Harlie hadn't invited him back to her room after lunch…

Logan and Victoria had taken turns watching the camera feeds from their room as they'd gotten ready for the evening's casual get-together.

He dried off and slung his towel over his shoulders before heading to the buffet table to fill his plate. Then juggling it, silverware, and a beer, he made his way to Victoria's lounger, where he sat at the end, not giving her any warning as he did so.

She jerked her feet away just in time to keep

them from being crushed. "I don't know where you put it," she grumbled, staring at his plate.

Logan shot her a grin. "Food is one of my pleasures. Workouts are a small price to pay."

She shook her head. "That plate is three meals for me."

"Go fill up a plate of your own."

She sighed and slid her feet off the chair. "Did you leave anything for the rest of us?"

He chuckled as she walked away.

"Heard there was some drama this morning," Pauline said as she took a seat beside him.

"No drama. Everything ended well," he said.

"Heard you were the hero of the day."

He raised his eyebrows. "I'm no hero. She just got a little excited when her brakes failed. She rescued herself."

Pauline shook her head. "She should be more careful. A lot of people are depending on her to show up on set."

"I'm sure she didn't intend to have any trouble with her ATV."

Her husband Cal arrived, carrying two plates. He handed one to Pauline then sat beside her. "Heard we missed some excitement."

Logan quickly took another bite of his meal so he didn't have to repeat the conversation he'd just had with Cal's wife.

Victoria returned, and he shifted to allow her

room to take her seat. Her plate held a healthy-sized portion of meat and a mound of salad. "You forgot to get a potato," he said. "They're coated in sesame oil and sea salt."

"I have plenty," she said, sounding a little snippy.

He raised his eyebrows and paid attention to his own plate.

The evening went on, music started up, and some danced. Alcohol was consumed. Harlie was the center of attention again but seemed a little less animated than the night before. He wondered if it was because of Adnan's disapproving presence or her assistant's sullen expression.

Again, he wondered why she put up with Adnan, but this time added her assistant to the list of people he found inconsistent with her personality.

When Victoria yawned, he didn't have to pretend to be the concerned fiancé; he tilted his head toward the patio doors. "Why don't you go on up? I'll be here a while." He darted a glance at his plate. "Seconds, you know."

She gave him a slight frown. Then her mouth tightened before relaxing again. She leaned closer to whisper in his ear. "Good idea, I guess. I can get some sleep, but you have to wake me up to keep an eye on the feeds later so you can rest."

He nodded. "Sure thing."

When she kissed his cheek, for just a second, he

thought it was real and nearly smiled. But then she tugged on his earlobe—a little too hard. Just a reminder that she was playacting.

When she strolled away, he felt a little disappointed.

Victoria showered and dressed in a pretty, silky pajama set she'd acquired for their junket. When she slipped under the covers, she remembered waking that morning spooned next to Logan.

It was so easy to forget this was just a job. That they were only work partners. Not a couple.

The more time she spent with him, the more she had to remind herself of that fact. Perhaps it was because this was a much lower-stress environment than she was accustomed to working in. She hated to admit it, but she was enjoying this assignment. And who wouldn't?

The food was good, and the location was amazing. The fact she was moving in such an elevated circle, with the beautiful and famous, was a fact she had to remind herself wasn't something she should get used to. Although, with Sadie's connections, they just might have the opportunity again, sometime.

She wondered what Harlie had planned for the next day and hoped it didn't involve anything with an engine. It was troubling to know someone here on the ranch had purposely sabotaged the actress's vehicle.

Why that might be so stumped her. Harlie wasn't the big star of the film. She was pretty and effervescent—not the typical, cliched spoiled starlet. She had boyfriend issues and didn't always think things through, but she wasn't a bad person. No one would put her on an enemy's list unless they were jealous of her trajectory as an actress or coveted her role.

Well, solving the mystery wasn't her and Logan's first order of business. Keeping her safe until filming started was. They'd called Jake while getting ready for the party to fill him in on what had transpired. Jake had promised to update Hank and told them to "holler" if they thought more operators should be assigned to the detail.

She reached for the lamp on the bedside table and turned off the light. Then she thought she ought to check the feeds before sleeping and slid out of bed to retrieve the tablet.

Nothing was happening in front of the house. Nothing to the side below Harlie's suite.

When she checked the feed at the barn area, all was quiet there, too. She hit the box anyway and rolled back the film. Nothing unusual had happened there.

Then she checked the feed on the second floor

outside Harlie's apartment and clicked to monitor the feed from the past hour.

Anita exited Harlie's room with an armload of towels then returned to her cart. Victoria was just about to click off the screen when she noted that Anita slid a phone from her apron's pocket, typed something, then glanced around.

Victoria wouldn't have thought anything of the action, except for that furtive glance the woman made. Like she was making sure she was alone. She looked…guilty. But of what?

Frowning, she thought about texting Logan, but Logan was keeping an eye on Harlie. It was probably nothing, but Victoria never ignored her intuition. And hers was buzzing that something was up.

She quickly changed into jeans and a dark top then twisted her hair up and clipped it to keep it out of the way. Then grabbing her lock pick kit—because, hey, who traveled without one?—she exited her room. She moved quickly to the stairs and up to the second floor. A glance down the hallway showed that it was clear. As well, the cart was gone, along with Anita.

Moving swiftly down the hallway, she drew her kit from her back pocket, glanced behind her to make sure she was still alone, then crouched next to the door and quickly unlocked it.

Once inside, she flicked on the foyer light. The room was cleaned, the bed made. Nothing seemed out of place, which was as it should be since Anita had just been there.

Maybe she'd been wrong. Maybe the furtive look was because Anita didn't want to be caught using her phone while working. Still, something didn't feel right.

She began scouting the rooms, starting in the sitting room, glancing under and behind furniture. She checked the kitchenette and refrigerator. A bottle of wine and several more bottles of sparkling water were there. She checked the bottles to see whether they'd been tampered with. Nothing.

Moving into the bathroom, she ran her hand over the top of the mirror, opened the shower door, picked up the toilet cover, and peered into the well. Nothing.

Then she moved into the bedroom, flicking on the overhead light. Again, she checked the closet and opened all the dresser drawers. She stood at the window and looked around the room, scanning methodically for anything that might be out of place.

A glint of light, perhaps a reflection on something very small, came from the base of the lamp on the dresser across from the bed.

She moved toward it, but guessing what it was, didn't look directly at it. Instead, she passed the dresser then pressed her back to the wall and reached behind the lamp. Her fingers caught on a very skinny cord.

Someone had set up a spy camera in Harlie's bedroom.

It had to have been Anita. But why? Was someone paying her to install it there? What were their intentions? Blackmail, perhaps? Who would care about who Harlie was sleeping with?

She shook her head, and then because she couldn't leave it there, she ripped the cord, balled it up in her fist, and left.

Back in her room, she kept checking the camera feed from outside Harlie's suite. She rolled it back to early that morning.

She watched as Adnan left the room, kissing Harlie at the doorway, and then walking away with a smile. She watched as a woman dressed in a housekeeping apron entered and left a few minutes later, her arms filled with laundry. Then she watched Harlie leave. Scrolling forward, she found Harlie returning after the ATV ride and then watched her depart for the party at the poolside.

Then Anita entered, spent about fifteen minutes inside, and departed, her arms filled with used towels.

She stored the feed to a file and shipped it to Jake with a note for him to have Swede find out what he could about Anita. Then she changed into her pajamas again and slipped into bed. She wasn't going to sleep, but she'd left the party ostensibly to do so and couldn't return, even though she was dying to pass this little tidbit along to Logan.

Instead, she texted him.

Hey.

Why aren't you asleep? Miss me?

Ha! I've been busy.

Without me? I'm hurt.

Victoria snorted.

Asshole. I saw something interesting on the feed.

Tell me.

Anita was acting squirrely outside Harlie's room.

Squirrely? Damn, I think I'm rubbing off on you. And?

I think she planted a camera.

You THINK?

Well, I FOUND a camera.

YOU WENT INTO HARLIE'S ROOM?!

Well, I didn't get caught. Had to check it out. Found a small spy camera. I'll show it to you when you get back here.

Damn. This party's dragging on.

We have to figure out who paid Anita to do it.

Cannot believe sweet Anita would do something like that.

She grinned, imagining him saying those words in his southern drawl.

Knucklehead.

Get some sleep if you can.

Will do.

Night.

After she exited the screen, she lay back and stared at the ceiling. She wondered if she fell asleep whether she'd awaken in his arms again. The thought didn't make her cringe. Not even a little bit.

What did it mean? That she was attracted? She huffed a breath. What woman wouldn't be? He was Grade-A wholesome, farm-raised man. She wondered how he'd wound up in the SEALs, seeing as how he was likely from some land-locked southern town. Likely Texas. Maybe Arkansas. She couldn't really place his accent, but then, he'd been a SEAL for a few years, so maybe the Navy had trimmed his drawl a bit.

After all the time they'd spent together over the last few days, how did she not know where he was from?

Maybe because she'd never asked. Should she have? They were partners. They ought to have traded some personal information. Maybe some war stories about their glory days with the SEALs and the FBI.

If she'd been a male, she had no doubt he would've been more forthcoming. He'd as much as admitted he wasn't used to working so closely with a female.

So, what was her excuse? She turned to her side and pounded her pillow to rearrange the feathers inside it. Only it was polyester foam, wasn't it?

She reached across for his pillow, sure it had to be more comfortable than hers. Then she drew it to her nose and inhaled. It smelled like him. His unique, manly smell, and maybe a hint of…cucumber? Had he used her shampoo?

Putting her pillow on his side of the bed, she clutched his to her chest and closed her eyes.

CHAPTER 8

"Hey, you stole my pillow."

Victoria cracked open one eye to glare at Logan. "Did not."

He bit back a grin. "Did so." He tugged it from under her head.

Letting out a huffed breath, she said, "How'd you even know? They're identical."

"Mine's softer."

Both eyes opened. "You tested them both before choosing yours, didn't you?"

He let his grin loose. "Damn straight. So, you're awake now?" He raised a single brow, liking that she hadn't moved away from him, even knowing he was sitting right beside her on her side of the mattress.

She shoved aside the covers and rubbed a hand over her face. "Yeah. Let me grab the tablet."

Logan watched as she strode toward the table wearing a flirty pajama set that looked almost as soft and silky as her long legs.

After retrieving her tablet, she returned to the bed, pushing her pillow against the headboard, and then sitting casually in front of him while she concentrated on bringing up the feed.

Logan fought not to let his gaze roam over her long bare legs or think about how her pretty top clung to the tips of her nipples. Her face was sleep-flushed, and her lips were a little swollen and pouty-looking. He wished he could kiss them to feel just how soft they were at that moment.

"Here," she said and thrust the tablet his way. Then she crossed her arms over her chest and frowned at him.

Had she caught him staring at her chest?

He cleared his throat and hit the play button. When he finished watching Anita, acting *squirrely*, he glanced back up at Victoria.

She reached to the side and balled her fist around something on the nightstand then dropped it on his palm.

After setting the tablet on the nightstand, he held up the end of the cable. "Yeah, it's a camera." Holding it closer, he looked for anything that might identify the manufacturer, which might help Swede search for who had purchased it, but no luck there.

He raised his eyebrows. "So, either someone's a

pervert and wanted to watch Harlie gettin' busy with her boyfriend, or maybe, the boyfriend is makin' sure he's the only one getting' busy with her…?"

"Or someone's looking to blackmail someone. But is it Harlie or Adnan they're trying to catch?" She blew out a breath. "I have no clue. But I did send the feed to Jake and asked him to get with Swede to do a deep dive on Anita. Maybe we can figure out if she was paid and by whom."

When she went silent, he glanced her way. Her expression was neutral, so he didn't have a clue what she was thinking about now.

He was thinking about how pretty she was—no makeup, her hair a little messy. She was close enough he could reach out, cup her shoulders, and bend toward her for that kiss he wanted.

Instead, he cleared his throat again and stood. "I'm gonna hit the shower."

She reached sideways for the tablet. "I'll keep an eye out."

"See if she had company tonight. I watched her head upstairs alone."

"Will do," she said, not glancing his way.

He went to his bag, which he still hadn't unpacked, and rifled through his clothing for a set of boxers. His hand hovered on a T-shirt, but he remembered waking that morning with her plastered against his chest, and he thought he'd enjoy it more if he forgot about the fucking tee.

Once inside the shower, he glanced down at his cock, which was semi-hard already. Boxers wouldn't hide it. So, he took himself in hand and closed his eyes, imagining a strong, long-fingered, feminine grip stroking him. Or better yet, her mouth opening to take him inside.

Fuck, why couldn't he think of her as his partner? He'd never wanted to fuck the guys he'd worked with. He should be more professional and compartmentalize his relationship with the woman who was slowly driving him nuts.

Everything about her turned him on. Even when she was snippy—hell, especially when she narrowed her eyes on him. Something inside him, something primitive, was challenged by her resistance.

I'm a sick fucker.

No, she was a fucking hot. Every slim, leanly muscled inch of her long body. And Lord above, her eyes had a way of looking at him that made him think she could read every one of his dirty thoughts. Her mouth…

That was all it took. His cock erupted, and he rubbed the orgasm out, his body swaying under the needle-like spray. When he finished washing up and dressed in his boxers, he felt more relaxed, more in control. Ready to slide between the sheets next to his partner and get some well-earned rest.

Until he opened the bathroom door and saw her head nodding on the *two* pillows she'd stacked beneath her. He'd bet anything his pillow was right beneath her cheek—and just like that, his arousal stirred again.

WHEN VICTORIA WOKE up the next morning, her chest was pressed against Logan's, and his thigh rested between hers. As well, his erection was impossible to ignore. In her sleep, her hand had cupped it. Still was. How the hell was she supposed to pull it away without waking him?

Thankfully, he was still breathing deeply, still unaware of her predicament.

For a moment, she actually savored that thought. Here she was with her hand on his dick. Maybe if she very gently moved her fingers a bit, she could satisfy her curiosity about it.

It was certainly firm. And thick. With a feather-like upward movement, she trailed her fingers upward, and then lay there feeling a little shocked by its length. *Holy fuck.*

Yeah, she needed to move away now—before her hormones kicked in and she made a mistake she couldn't walk back.

So, pretending she was still asleep, she closed

her eyes and dragged her hand away, raising it above her head to stretch, like she was only beginning to wake up. For added satisfaction, she smacked his cheek as she moved her hand and then jerked. "Oh, sorry," she said and began to wiggle away.

Only she hadn't noted where his hands were when she'd moved.

One rested on her ass. The other cradled her back. He drew a deep breath and tightened his arms, bringing her closer to his chest. His thigh slid between hers, moving upward to bump against her crotch.

She opened one eye and discovered he was fully awake and grinning right back at her. His hips flexed, crowding his cock against her lower belly. "Don't stop now."

"I was asleep. I didn't know what I was doing."

"You've been awake for a few minutes now. Didn't stop you from feelin' me up."

"Was not."

His eyes narrowed. "Really?"

She swallowed hard, knowing she'd been caught. Her cheeks filled with heat. So did other parts of her anatomy she refused to acknowledge. "Well, I'm awake now. And we really should check on our girl."

"I did twenty minutes ago. She's still in her room. No one's stirrin'. It's early." The hand on her ass moved slowly, his fingers spreading to cover more area. "Do you always wake up horny?"

Her jaw sagged. Then her blood boiled. She slid a hand down to cup his hardness. "Do you?"

His breath whistled between his teeth. "Careful there. Don't start somethin' you can't finish."

"Can't?" she arched an eyebrow, even knowing he was pricking her competitive side now. But he was right. She had woken up horny—and it was all his fault. Why shouldn't she expect him to do something about it? Her fingertips traced his length again. "So, I was curious. Shoot me."

"I don't mind you *satisfyin'* your curiosity, Vicky," he murmured.

Despite the fact his deepening tone was doing things to her, she wrinkled her nose. "I hate that nickname."

His one-sided smile said he'd guessed that already. He moved the hand from her ass to cover hers against his dick, and he slid it up and down. "I won't mind if you take a peek."

"I've seen dicks before," she said breathlessly, fighting the urge to curve her fingers around him.

He lifted her hand and sucked in a breath before sliding both their hands inside his boxers.

Oh, fucking Jesus. The head of his cock was broad and cushiony, and there was moisture in the center. He pushed her hand downward, smoothing it over the long, steamy column, all the way down until her palm cupped his balls. Then his fingers tightened on her so that she gave him a squeeze.

"Satisfied?" he whispered.

Not even a little bit. She bit her lower lip to stifle a groan.

"Decision time," he said, his voice sounding a little tighter. Maybe it was because she was still gripping his balls, her fingers tugging and cuddling them. She hadn't even noticed she was doing it or that his hand no longer controlled hers.

Decision time. Was there any going back? Could they ignore this little…episode? She didn't think she could. She'd be distracted for the rest of the day. "Maybe…we should just get this over with…?" she said, striving to keep her voice from sounding small and breathy.

"Think we both might have a hard time keepin' our heads in the game if we don't?"

She nodded eagerly, glad he was following her train of thought. "Yeah. That."

"You sure?"

She blew out a breath between her pursed lips and nodded again. Only, she didn't want to be the one to initiate this, although she guessed she already had. She wanted him to take the lead. Just as a salve to her pride, so she'd know he was as eager as she was to…get this out of their systems, so to speak.

Abruptly, he rolled away. "Strip."

He shoved down his boxers and gave her a hard stare.

She pulled her pajama top over her head, ignoring the buttons because that would take too long. Then she shoved the bottoms down.

He pushed aside the sheet and coverlet. Something she hadn't thought about. Now, he could see everything. But so could she.

He was everything her fingers had already "seen."

"Stop lookin' at it, and for fuck's sake don't touch it."

She couldn't help letting out a nervous laugh. "Or what?"

"Or I'll blow before you're ready."

"Oh." She licked her lower lip and forced herself to raise her gaze to meet his.

His mouth twitched at one corner. "You look at it like you looked at my potato last night."

She wrinkled her nose and laughed. "What? Your…penis…looks nothing like your potato did."

"But you wanted it. I'll bet you were salivating over it."

She lifted her chin. "Think I'm salivating over your…penis?"

He grimaced. "I really hate that word. Call it a dick. Call it a spike, a post, meat—just not that."

Now, he was grinning. Which she found so attractive, and which also relieved some of the pressure she'd been feeling a moment ago while staring at his…dick.

"How do we do this?" she whispered.

He moved closer, coming up on an elbow to lean over her. "Don't you know?"

"I…don't want to wait."

"Ah. Then give me a second…" He moved away and rolled off the bed onto his feet. Going to his duffle, he rooted inside his toiletry kit and held up a long strip of condoms.

"Now, I'm wondering if you planned on this to happen," she grumped.

"I never travel without. You never know." His eyebrows waggled as he strode back to her, taking his time, likely so she could admire the way his cock bobbed.

Damn, it stood at a 45-degree angle from his body. "Um, it's…impressive," she said, then tossed back her hair like she felt more confident than she did at the moment.

"*It's* inspired."

She pressed her lips together then let loose another laugh. "Just get *it* over here." And then she opened her arms.

Logan climbed onto the bed and right over her, his weight braced on his hands. "I want to kiss every sweet inch of you, Vic."

"Later. Please. I don't want to wait."

When he lowered his hips, she was ready, her legs parted, knees rising.

He nudged against her entrance, and she noted his jaw tightening, his features hardening as he tried to take his time.

But she was more than ready and wouldn't mind a little painful stretching. Reaching around him, she dug her fingernails into his buttocks. "All of it. Now."

His thrust was steady and unrelenting. When he was fully seated inside her, he dipped his head to kiss her mouth. "We forgot a few steps."

"Didn't forget a thing. We got straight to the point. I like your point."

His mouth stretched, and he kissed her hard before glancing down between their bodies. Then he began to move. "Now, isn't that a sight?" he murmured, his voice husky.

She lifted her head to glance downward then moaned. "I can't believe you can stuff all that inside me."

"Huh. Not the least bit romantic, are you?"

"I'm…out of words, Logan." She didn't want to talk. Or tease. Or admire. She wanted him to fuck her. Hard. "Move," she ordered, digging her nails into his backside.

He hissed between his teeth then moved with purpose, gliding inward, sliding out—slowly at first, which irritated the shit out of her. She supposed he had a reason; he was large and her vagina felt pretty crowded. But she loved it. Every single inch of *it*.

When her body released more moisture, he pumped faster, his thrusts jarring her body. She had to let go of his ass and brace her palms against the headboard to keep him from hammering her up the bed.

Soon, the bed creaked, their breaths panted, and the sounds they made below were slick and nasty.

Logan leaned on one arm and slid his hand down her belly to finger her clit. "Babe, I'm almost there. Come with me."

She moaned as his finger rasped her tender flesh. Then she felt the tension tighten. Her back arched hard, her legs straightened, and she let them fall open as far as she could, wanting to feel him crash fully, deeply against her. Suddenly, the tension inside her unfurled, catapulting her over the crest of an orgasm that felt so powerful she couldn't see anything but flashes of gold.

Slowly, she came back to herself and realized he was rocking gently against her, doing his best to prolong her orgasm. When she blinked up at him, he smiled then cupped the side of her face and kissed her.

CHAPTER 9

LOGAN FOUND himself growing jealous as the zipline operator adjusted the harness around Victoria's waist and thighs. Logan had adjusted his own, frowning at the man when he'd stepped forward to tighten his straps.

When the operator had seen his expression, he'd laughed and held up his hands. "Looks like you know what you're doing, man."

As they began the climb up the ladder to the platform above, he kept below Victoria, admiring the flex of the muscles in her legs and ass as she ascended the wooden steps, following closely behind Harlie.

Making love to Victoria hadn't gotten a thing out of his system. He wanted more. Now that he knew how it felt to run his hands over her silky skin and sink into her depths, he feared he was hooked. He was pretty sure she felt the same way, too. He'd caught her giving him sideways glances throughout breakfast, and when he'd placed his hand on her thigh to give her a quick, reassuring squeeze, just to connect with her again, she'd slid her hand over his and laced their fingers together.

It was odd. He'd felt a rush of pride at the thought that this beautiful woman wanted his attention.

The 186-feet climb took them up to an open platform with guardrails around it. The cable they'd slide down was secured to a beam in the roof, and a gate opened on one side to allow the rider to exit the platform and "zip" down the line which took them over and then through the forest, ending at an artificial lake where they landed in the water and against inflated guards.

Before heading out for the morning's adventure, Logan had done a quick internet search to check out the reviews and see whether there had been any safety issues, but was reassured by what he'd read. Any saboteur wouldn't know when Harlie, in particular, would be sailing down the line, and they'd have to compromise the three cheerful employees who saw to the safety of the customers coming up the ladder. Not likely in the least.

So, he'd keep an eye out for trouble but enjoy watching Victoria on her "virgin" experience. She'd admitted over breakfast this wasn't something she'd ever tried.

"Not afraid of heights?" he asked, standing close behind her.

"Nope. I'm good."

"Some folks don't like the speed."

"No problems there either."

"Not nervous at all?"

She shot a glare over her shoulder. "Are you trying to make me nervous?"

He settled his hands on her shoulders. "Not at all. Just wanted you to know I'd be right behind you."

"Since they don't let us bunch up on the way down, you won't even see me until we're at the end."

She turned her head toward him again and looked at his mouth.

Invitation enough. He gave her a quick kiss. When he pulled back, she smiled and quickly looked forward again.

He was smiling, too.

Cal Gross was the first one to step toward the edge of the platform. A carabiner was attached to the harness, and then clipped to the trolley. Then he was instructed to hold onto the handlebars and jump off the platform.

Cal aimed a smile at Harlie that looked more like a grimace then faced forward and leaped.

He hooted as he descended, whirring out of sight.

Next was Harlie, who gave the operator a confident smile. She held out her hand for the carabiner and connected herself, waiting while he checked her harness and had her test her weight against the pulley on the wire before walking her toward the edge. When he gave her a thumbs-up, she took a couple of steps back, and then ran to the edge. Her laughter followed her out of sight.

Next was Victoria, who let the operator clip her to the pulley. She grabbed the handlebars and walked sedately toward the edge. There, she glanced back, gave him a wink, then bounded outward, zipping down the line.

The operator gave Logan a glance, and he arched an eyebrow. "I've done this a time or two."

"Bet you have." He stood back and let Logan affix the carabiner, test his weight in the seat harness, then walk by himself to the edge. He leaped out and smiled, feeling free like a bird, as he felt the initial drop then sped down the line, the trees beneath him blurring.

As he went lower, the trees parted, and the line swept him past the upper branches, down and down. He'd missed this feeling. Almost like stepping out of an airplane at 12,000 feet. Feeling the chute open and jerk him upward, then floating downward.

Too soon, the trees fell away and the lake appeared, the water looking like blue glass beneath him. Then he was nearing the end and braced for the impact, his feet dragging in the water until he hit the inflated barrier at the end. It gently knocked the wind out of him, and he let go a laugh as he sank partway into the water.

An operator on the ground stepped around to unhook him and give him a hand onto a platform behind the barrier. There he met Victoria, Cal, and Harlie, who all wore huge grins.

"That was so much fun!" Victoria said, jumping up and down.

He grabbed her hands and jumped up and down with her, feeling silly, but also enjoying her giddiness. The others just grinned at them.

After the rest of their party completed their rides, they headed back to the vehicles to take them back to the ranch. Harlie rode with Cal and another of her friends. Adnan was behind the wheel, his expression neutral, but Logan had seen the relief on his face when she'd walked into view.

The man didn't have much of a poker face when it came to his feelings for Harlie. Logan almost felt sorry for him.

Seated in the back of an SUV beside Victoria, he

kept his arm around her, and she laid her head on his shoulder. She was still smiling.

"Have you ever sky-dived?" he asked.

She nodded. "I went through the training, but I can't say it was something I enjoyed. All the way down, I kept imagining every single thing that could go wrong with my chute."

"Zip-lining was a cakewalk for you then."

"Yeah, it was pretty fun." She glanced sideways at him. "You seemed to know your way around up there."

"I hadn't done it in a really long time. Used to do it when I was a kid."

"Really?"

He nodded. "I'd go camping with a group of guys. We'd do some huntin', fishin', and we always spent our last day on a zipline. Nothin' as high as that one, but it was fun."

"Where was that? You've never said where you were from…"

"Oklahoma. A small-town east of Oklahoma City."

"Do you have family there?"

"I do. Mom and Dad are still kickin'. I've also got a brother and a sister. They're both married. He's a deputy. She's the mayor now."

She wrinkled her nose. "You didn't want to head back there after your service?"

"I know I could've been hired into the sheriff's department, but… I don't know. After some of the stuff I've seen…done…the thought of spendin' my days in a cruiser just didn't appeal."

"Huh."

He arched an eyebrow. "What?"

"Nothing. Just…huh."

He chuckled. "I know you have more to say."

She turned her head to gaze into his face. "You're an adrenaline junkie. Tell the truth. You'd have been bored driving in that cruiser."

He rolled his eyes and sighed. "Yeah. I did a ride-along one night with my brother when I was on leave. I ended up sleepin' in the backseat."

She chuckled. "I know you've done surveillance in your line of work. How do you stand it?"

"I used to run scenarios in my head. Figure out all the shit that could go sideways and how I'd counter the threat." He turned his head to glance down at her. "How about you? What did you do for fun when you were a kid?"

"I was raised in a little town in Virginia, near Washington, D.C. We'd drive to Virginia Beach and spend the day in the water—riding jet skis or swimming. Must sound kind of lame to a SEAL."

"Not at all. When I was going through training in San Diego, I spent my weekends surfin', fishin' off a dock, and swimmin'. It was a world away from Oklahoma."

"Fishing seems to be something you like to do a lot."

"It is. It's…relaxin'."

"But not fly-fishing."

He grimaced. "It looks a little fruity to me."

She giggled. "Fruity?"

"Yeah, all that gear, all that slow-mo castin'. Wavin' your pole around…"

She snickered again. "But *fruity*? How very un-PC of you."

He shrugged. "Don't know how else to describe it. Don't know a guy I grew up with who'd fish like that. Not even the girls." Yes, he was exaggerating. And he'd be game to give it a try, but he liked seeing her laugh.

"I've never fished."

He dropped his jaw, pretending shock. "Not once?"

"Nope. My dad is a sociology professor. My mom, a city planner. Growing up, they were either busy at their jobs or supporting some political cause. I was on my own so far as recreation was concerned. My friends preferred to spend their time in the mall being seen."

"Now, that doesn't sound like you."

"It wasn't. Oh, I'd go occasionally, but I thought it was all a waste of time and money. I played soccer. Was in the National Honor Society. Spent weekends cleaning up cat and dog poop at the

Humane Society…"

"How'd you end up in the FBI?"

"On Career Day at my high school, an FBI agent came to speak. He was the father of one of the students. Everything he talked about sounded so exciting to me. I took home the pamphlets of information he left and plotted out everything I needed to do to qualify. I studied criminal justice in college, worked out hard, spent weekends at the firing range. My dad thought I was nuts, but I was determined. Right after graduation, I applied, and luckily, I was accepted."

"No luck to it."

She nodded. "You're right. No luck at all."

"So, why'd you leave?" he asked, keeping his voice low.

She glanced out the window and didn't speak for a long moment.

He thought maybe he'd stepped over a line, but she blew out a breath and turned in her seat to face him.

"I spent time undercover. Probably too many years. My last assignment didn't end well. My partner was shot. Everything went sideways. We didn't get our target—the head of a big crime organization. Sure, we arrested many of their leaders, but we didn't take it all the way down. When I met with my handler, I told him I was done."

"So, you just walked away?"

She shrugged. "I wanted something…else. Something that didn't leave me feeling…dirty."

Logan understood the feeling. He leaned his forehead against hers. "Babe, I get it. I'm right there with you."

CHAPTER 10

Victoria spent the rest of the day feeling as though she was walking on a cloud. The morning had been fun—the ride home, revelatory. Not just because she'd learned some new things about her partner, but because they seemed to share more in common than not.

They were both looking for a life beyond the one they'd lived. They'd both suffered losses. Plus, every time he touched her, she felt as though her body and her soul were uplifted.

A sentiment she would have scoffed at before today. But there was something about him, and about herself, that somehow combined to become *more* when they were together.

Was this what love felt like?

She was heading to the stables at that moment while Logan was making a call to Swede at Hank's office to see what he'd learned about Anita. Harlie was going for a late afternoon ride, this time on horseback, despite how it "weakened" her thighs.

When she'd said that over lunch, Adnan had winced a bit, but hadn't given his full-blown usual frown. Progress, Victoria guessed. Harlie would wear down his stuffiness if she got half a chance. She wondered if Harlie was doing it on purpose.

That would mean that Harlie was smarter than those around her thought she was.

Trevor Hanson, her movie co-star, had rolled into lunch, his hair a little disheveled, perhaps by design, but had made a face when they'd mentioned riding. "It would be just my luck to get thrown by a horse and break something, days before filming starts." Then he'd given Harlie a pointed stare, which she'd only shrugged off.

Elaine, her assistant, begged off too, saying something about needing to work on social media posts.

Horses were being brought out of the barn onto the hardpacked dirt area in front, fully saddled. Everyone was standing back as Harlie made the first selection.

Emmet, the foreman, led a gelding out. The horse was a gorgeous buckskin, and of course, Harlie clapped her hands, decision made.

As she approached the horses and the men holding their reins, Victoria had her first misgivings. She wished she'd let the Oklahoma boy take this ride. She'd had lessons on an English saddle when she'd been a teenager, but this was different. And it had been years since she'd sat on a horse.

Somehow, the animals looked taller than she remembered.

The British cowboy she'd met the evening she and Logan had arrived gave her a wink as she moved closer to the group. "This girl's nice and gentle. She has a hard mouth, too, so you'll have to pull harder on her reins than you'd think." He waggled his eyebrows. "You have ridden before…?"

The tone he used as he asked the question was an unsubtle flirtation. She gave him a wide-eyed stare. "I've ridden many times," she said, blinking innocently.

He chuckled and held out the reins. "Need a hand up?"

The horse was tall, so unless she wanted to do the splits to get her toe into the stirrup, she'd need help. She gave him a nod and waited as he bent with his hands cupped then lifted her into the air.

"I'll adjust these stirrups," he said, reaching under the stirrup fender.

"They feel fine," she said after she placed her boots in them.

He arched an eyebrow. "You've ridden an English saddle."

"Yeah?" she said, not understanding his point.

"You need the stirrup to be longer on a Western saddle. You'll be sitting differently. More forward."

She wrinkled her nose but took his word for it, and waited as he adjusted the stirrups. When she placed her boots in them again, the length felt wrong, but she figured she'd get the hang of it. The saddle itself felt huge.

She nudged the mare's sides with her boots and walked her around to where Harlie was mounting her horse. Harlie's attention was on Adnan.

Victoria understood why. Adnan looked completely at home atop his horse. In command. Confident. And he was smiling—which made him extremely handsome.

He pulled up alongside Harlie once she was fully seated. "As always, you may lead the way."

Harlie tilted her head. "Not always," she said softly.

Which made his smile widen.

Victoria was sure that comment held some sexual undertones because Harlie was blushing now.

The English cowboy joined them, seated on his own palomino. "Welcome, everyone. I think you'll enjoy the trails this afternoon, and Anita is organizing a picnic along the way."

There were cheers, and then the Brit waved an arm toward the gate being held open by another ranch hand.

Victoria's phone vibrated in the pocket of her snap-button shirt. It was Logan.

"Hey," she said. "We're leaving in just a few minutes. You finish with your calls?"

"I have one more, but I'm pretty sure I can find you all. What direction are you heading?"

She glanced toward the Brit. "Logan's going to try to catch up. Which direction are we heading?"

"East, mostly," he said.

"Heard that," Logan said. "Later."

As soon as she put her phone away, Harlie and the Brit led their little "posse" out the gate, and they were on their way.

Victoria studied the way the Brit rode and was soon "rolling" comfortably in her own seat. At least it felt so at the moment. She was sure she'd be pretty sore by the end of the ride because it had been so many years since she'd been atop a horse.

The Brit slowed his pace and pulled in beside her. "Was I correct about the stirrups?"

"You were."

"You look natural in a saddle."

His gaze swept her with a little too much famil-iarity. To distract him, she murmured, "You said there would be a picnic somewhere along the way. How long will we be riding? Some of these folks will be pretty sore if they're on a horse for too long."

"A couple of hours, maybe. And they can take

the bus back if they don't want to return via horseback."

"Bus?"

He smiled. "Yeah, we expect most, if not all, the riders will be ready for a soak in a hot tub after they get back. We'll string the horses together and bring them back to the barn for them."

"All the amenities," she said, shaking her head.

"We do aim to please." Then with another waggle of his eyebrows, he kicked his horse into a faster pace to retake the lead.

There were eight along for the ride. Victoria rode in the middle of the nose-to-tail entourage. At first, the pace was sedate while riders grew accustomed to their saddles and their horses.

She rode a little to the left of the trail to keep an eye on the three in front.

Harlie was talking to the Brit, one hand gesticulating while the other controlled her reins. For once, Adnan wasn't watching her closely. His attention was on the mountains on either side of the valley.

She wondered how different this was for him and whether he'd ridden much in Saudi Arabia. She'd seen pictures of Arabian horses running in the desert but could only imagine the contrasts Adnan was noting—green forests, blue and white peaks rather than red sandstone formations.

It was also very different from her experience

riding on trails through the gently rolling hills in Virginia.

Up ahead, Harlie laughed, drawing her attention. Her horse shot forward with Harlie bent over its neck. Adnan kicked his horse into a gallop to follow as did the Brit.

Victoria blew out a deep breath and did the same, following in the dust the three riders left, passing Cal and Pauline who were frowning.

"That's just reckless," Pauline called out. "We should stay together."

"You do that," Victoria said over her shoulder. "You'll catch up." She added under her breath, "Eventually."

LOGAN deep-sixed the lazy ride Emmet recommended in favor of a younger horse that looked built for speed.

"I'm from Oklahoma," Logan said, and it was enough of an explanation that Emmet tipped his hat and pointed in the direction the riders had left twenty minutes ago.

He'd quickly found the fresh tracks they'd left in the dirt. The thoroughbred he rode seemed to know the path quite well, so he loosened the reins to let the horse do what he was born to do.

Soon enough, he came up on the rear of a line

of horses. He passed the first riders then paused beside Cal. "Have you seen Victoria?"

Cal rolled his eyes. "She's trying to keep up with Harlie. That girl's determined to break her own neck."

Logan gave the man a quick smile then gave his horse a nudge of encouragement, and off they went again.

Logan was wondering if he'd ever catch up to the group when he came to a low ridge and glanced down to see four horses and riders. He clucked to his mount and leaned back in the saddle as the horse began the descent down the other side.

Soon enough, he pulled up beside Victoria. Harlie was giving her horse a bit of a rest up ahead or he might not have caught them so quickly.

Logan eyed Victoria in her saddle. "How's your—"

"If you were about to say ass—"

"Not what I was about to say, but since you mentioned it..." He gave her an exaggerated leer, which made her grin back at him.

She wrinkled her nose. "My ass is feeling a little tenderized."

"I can give you a massage when we get back..."

"I heard that!" Harlie called out and laughed.

Victoria rolled her eyes. "Don't encourage her."

"Heard that, too!"

Up ahead the trees gave way to a meadow. A bus

was parked along a dirt road. Tables had been set up, and several hands, plus Anita, were readying two tables erected end to end and covered with a red-checkered tablecloth with glasses, plates, and cutlery. As they dismounted and handed their reins to the cowboys standing by to assist them, large baskets were retrieved from the bus and carried to the tables.

Logan glanced back down the trail they'd just traveled on and saw the first of the riders from the slower group approaching.

Anita gave Logan a tight smile and ignored Victoria. "We're serving fried chicken with potato salad, baked beans, and coleslaw, and there will be pies for dessert. There's a trashcan filled with ice and cold sodas. Help yourselves to a drink then have a seat."

Victoria leaned sideways into Logan's arm. "Wonder if she knows we removed that camera."

Logan shrugged. "We haven't seen her back inside that room. Could mean she's not aware—"

"Which would mean she was only paid to set it up," she finished for him. "Not part of the plan."

He liked that they seemed to be on the same wavelength, finishing each other's sentences. It made for more efficient sharing of information in his mind.

They both took a seat across and slightly down from Harlie. Adnan sat beside the actress.

Cal and Pauline, who'd just left their horses with the cowboys, were quick to take seats directly across from the couple.

"Lord, I won't be able to sit straight for a week," Pauline said with a groan.

Harlie grinned. "You can always take the bus back to the ranch."

Pauline glanced at Cal who grimaced. "I think we both will."

From Victoria's expression, she might've been half-hoping Harlie would take that route, too, but Harlie smiled at Adnan. "You game to ride back to the ranch house?"

Adnan's smile was doting—and a little superior. "If you wish it…"

Harlie glanced around the other riders. "Anyone else coming?"

Victoria smiled. "I'm game. I didn't know how much I've missed riding."

Logan nodded. "I'm in, too."

Harlie glanced at the Brit who tipped his cowboy hat. "Guess that makes five of us. Better eat up, Logan and Vicky. We need to get back on the trail, or we won't make it back before dark."

Logan smothered a smile as Victoria bristled at the nickname, all the while keeping her smile in place. He passed the plate of chicken and held up the tongs. "Breast or chicken wing?"

Her eyes narrowed. "Is that code for something?" she muttered.

"It's just chicken."

She huffed a breath. "I'll take a breast."

"So will I, sweetheart," he whispered. "When we get back…"

"You two are just too cute," Harlie said.

"Men do not know how to whisper," Victoria said.

"I whisper just fine," Logan said dryly.

Adnan's gaze met Logan's, and he winked. Logan couldn't help it. He was starting to like the guy.

CHAPTER 11

THIS TIME with Logan's help mounting her horse, Victoria only winced a little as she pulled the reins to turn her horse to head back down the trail they'd already traveled.

Again, Harlie set the pace, but she seemed happy to keep a slower pace, riding side by side with Adnan.

The couple seemed… Victoria didn't quite have the right word to describe it, but they seemed more in synch. More comfortable around each other. She wasn't sure when they would have reached this state, because she'd been watching Harlie's room and he hadn't been there again after the first night, but perhaps just being in each other's company was helping them relax with one another.

Kind of like her and Logan. They, too, rode side by side a little distance away from the other couple.

They could hear their voices but not make out their words. The distance afforded some privacy.

The Brit trailed behind Logan and Victoria, and after a pointed stare from Logan, hadn't tried to catch up to join their conversation.

"So, you like Adnan," Victoria murmured.

"Yeah, I don't think he means her any harm or would spy on her. Nor do I think he's behind the incidents on the set. I don't know when he would have had the opportunity."

She frowned. "I'm still curious why she thought he tried to kidnap her in Costa Rica."

"Are we sure that really happened?" Logan asked. "Harlie mentioned it to Sadie, but could it have just been…"

"Exaggeration? Drama?"

He shrugged. "She is an actress."

Victoria wrinkled her nose. "She's reckless, and maybe a little immature, but she doesn't seem like she'd lie about something like that."

"We need to hear it first-hand from her."

"You mean, I do," she said.

He wrinkled his nose. "Yeah, I don't think she'd confide in me."

Victoria let her head fall back and groaned. "I'm *sooo* not the kind of woman other women confide in—unless they're in danger or want to rat someone else out. I'm not… I don't…" Her shoulders sank. "I'm not good at talking with other women. Most of my professional life has been spent in the company of men."

"You seem to have at least four women you get along really well with."

"That's because they're like me." She glanced sideways at him. "We're not…" She blew out a frustrated breath. "You know, I don't usually have these kinds of problems communicating, but girl-talk is outside my wheelhouse."

"Do you think it might be time to let her know why we're really here?" he asked softly.

"We should wait. Nothing's happened. I mean, other than the hole in the fuel line of her ATV—and that camera being placed inside her room." Victoria frowned. "I don't like the idea of that. All by itself, it's such an invasion of privacy."

"It's your call."

"I'll think about it."

Ahead, Harlie laughed and reached out to smack Adnan's arm. Then she widened her legs and brought her boots against her horse's sides, causing it to pick up speed.

"Here we go again," Victoria muttered.

They joined the chase. She had to admit it; now that she felt comfortable in this particular saddle, she was enjoying herself. Watching Logan beside her, she could tell he was as well. He looked damn good in his cowboy clothes.

Ahead, she heard a shrill cry, and then watched

as Harlie seemed to slide sideways on her horse. Only, it wasn't just her—her saddle was shifting, too. There was nothing to be done to help her. Adnan moved his horse away as she fell, kicking out of her stirrups and then landing hard on the ground. The horse continued galloping down the trail.

Victoria and Logan slowed. Logan leaped out of his saddle and ran to her, settling on his knees beside Harlie and Adnan who'd been similarly as agile. Victoria was slower, but she dropped the reins of her horse as she ran toward the three. Behind her came the sound of the Brit's boots moving swiftly.

"Harlie," Adnan said softly, reaching out to her.

Harlie's face was panicked, and she looked as though she couldn't breathe. She'd had the wind knocked out of her. Realizing her predicament, Adnan bent over her, placed his lips on hers, and blew.

A moment later, she shoved at his shoulders to get him to move back and she lay there, gasping for breath. "What the fuck?" she said, her voice a creaky squeal.

"Are you hurt?" Adnan asked, his hands still extended, like he was afraid to touch her.

Logan moved around her and squatted beside the saddle. His gaze went to Victoria, and she knew there was trouble.

Harlie got her elbows beneath her and frowned. Slowly, she moved her legs, and then rolled to her side then her stomach and pushed off the ground, accepting Adnan's hand when she stood.

"Are you sure you should move?" he asked.

"I don't think anything's broken," she whispered, then held up her elbow and stared at it. Blood was beginning to seep into the material of her shirt.

Logan pulled a knife from the scabbard he wore on his belt and handed it to Adnan who cut away her sleeve then cursed. Her skin was scraped and cut.

"Pauline's going to have a conniption," Harlie said.

"We should get you home and into a tub," Adnan said. "Maybe we should take you to a hospital for x-rays—"

"No fucking way. This is…nothing."

Adnan's eyebrows lowered. "You probably have some deep bruising."

"Which makeup will cover," she said, her lower lip pouting. "If Sadie hears about this, she'll be all over my ass. She gave me strict orders to keep out of trouble. They don't want any delays."

"Your health is more important, love."

"My career is on the line with this movie," she said. "I have to be ready from day one." She wrestled her arm away from him and took a step back. "I'm okay. It was just a stupid accident."

"The second one today," Adnan said, his voice biting.

Logan's gaze cut to Victoria's. From his look, this was anything but an accident. But now wasn't the time to tell Harlie about that. They needed to speak to her alone.

She shook her head and stepped toward Harlie. "Should we wait until the ranch can send an ATV to pick you up, or do you think you can ride back?"

Harlie scowled as she looked down the trail. "My horse is long gone."

"You can ride with me," Adnan said.

Harlie's mouth tightened.

Victoria gave her a small smile. "You can ride my horse if you like. I can ride back with Logan."

"Thank you," Harlie said, then moved past Adnan, displaying a little bit of a limp as she went to Victoria's horse.

"I'll take care of all of this," the cowboy said, indicating toward the saddle.

Logan's gaze landed on the Brit and narrowed. "We'll keep the pace slow. Don't want any more accidents."

"Good idea," the cowboy said.

Once they were on their way again, Harlie and Adnan in front, Adnan riding close and wearing a very worried frown, Victoria leaned toward Logan's ear. "Okay, so what's up?"

"Her girth strap was cut."

"Not frayed?"

"No. Cut. More than three-quarters of the way through. Had to have happened while we ate."

Victoria blew out a frustrated breath. "It could have been anyone. One of Harlie's crew or Adnan…"

"Or Anita or any of the cowboys out there to lend a hand."

She sighed. "We have to warn Harlie."

"I agree."

They were quiet the rest of the way back.

THEY TOOK turns showering as one of them kept watch on the monitors to see when Harlie left her suite. Adnan had accompanied her inside but left ten minutes later, his face dark and his brows lowered.

Victoria showered first. Then she quickly dressed while Logan bathed. When he exited the bathroom fully dressed, she was ready. They headed straight for Harlie's suite.

Logan rapped his knuckles on the door.

"Gimme a minute," came a muffled voice. A moment later, Harlie, rubbing moisture from her hair with a towel blinked in surprise seeing them there. "If you're here to check on me, I'm okay. I'm just a little banged up. Believe me, I've had worse."

"We need to talk," Logan said.

Harlie's expression changed. She lost her usual bravado, and her eyes widened. "All right." She stepped back and let them pass through the door. "I suppose you've already been in touch with Sadie. What'd she say? Did she fire me? I did promise to stay safe…"

Victoria held up a hand. "We haven't talked to her. Not yet. Please sit. We need to talk."

Harlie waved them toward the loveseat, and she took the armchair across from it. "So, what's this all about?" Her blue eyes had lost their initial fearful gleam. Now, her expression was set.

Victoria looked to Logan who gave a shrug, telling her silently that she could handle this. She met Harlie's guarded stare. "I'm not a physical trainer. And Logan's not working for the production team."

Harlie stiffened in her seat. "You lied? Are you paparazzi?" Then her eyebrows lowered. "Sadie vouched for you both."

"And Sadie would never betray you," Victoria said. "We're with the Brotherhood Protectors. Do you know what that is?"

Harlie nodded slowly. "Heard about it from Sadie. She's very proud of the agency Hank has set up. Some sort of bodyguard service—Wait! You're bodyguards?" She leaned forward in her chair, her eyebrows lowering. "She thought I needed babysitting?" she said, her tone rising slightly.

"Harlie, it's not just about you," Logan said, his voice gruff. He bent forward, resting his forearms on his thighs and clasping his hands in front of him. "Security on the set has been tightened, too. There've been some incidents out there, too. Possible sabotage." He went on the list of incidents while Harlie's expressive face moved through a range of emotions. "And after what happened in Costa Rica—"

Harlie held up a hand. "I told Sadie that in confidence. Besides, I don't think Adnan had anything to do with it."

Logan's gaze locked on her. "We need to know exactly what happened in Costa Rica."

Harlie pushed up from her seat and began pacing. "This isn't anyone's business but mine. Nothing happened. Adnan swore he didn't know anything about it—"

"Harlie," Victoria said, her voice sharpening. "Someone cut the strap on your saddle today. You sliding off your horse was not an accident."

"Neither was the hole poked in your ATV's brake line," Logan said.

Harlie's jaw dropped, and she stopped pacing and took her seat. "Someone did those things…on purpose?"

"Yes, Harlie," Victoria said softly. "And there's more."

Harlie rubbed a hand over her face then straightened in her chair. "All right. What else?"

Victoria pulled the bundle of cord from her pocket and held it out to Harlie.

"What's this?" Harlie said, holding it up to look at it.

"The night we arrived, Logan and I set up surveillance cameras around this place. One was planted in the hallway outside your room."

"You've been spying on me?"

Victoria held up her hand. "Let me finish. While you were still outside at the pool with your friends last night, I observed one of the staff entering and leaving your room. Something about her didn't feel…right. So, I searched your room. I found that. It was planted near the base of the lamp on the desk across from your bed."

"Someone set up a spy camera to watch me in bed?" Harlie said, her voice tightening into a squeak.

"Yes. But I removed it. And we've monitored everyone going in and out of your rooms since then."

Harlie's breaths were faster now. Victoria was afraid she'd start to hyperventilate, so she rose and knelt beside Harlie, reaching out for her hand.

"We're here to keep you safe. We'll try as well to figure out who's doing this."

"It's not Adnan," Harlie said quickly.

"We don't think so either," Logan said quickly. "He was sincerely shocked when you slid off that horse today."

"But who…?"

"We don't know, but we thought you should be aware that someone means you or the film harm. We're going to stick closer to you going forward."

Harlie's gaze went around the room as she drew deeper breaths. "I want to tell Adnan."

Victoria glanced at Logan who shrugged.

"All right," Victoria said, "but we'd like to be there. He might know something. Maybe he's not involved, but we have to look at this from every angle. We'll need to treat everyone here as a possible threat from here on out."

Harlie let out a strangled laugh. "He's going to love this. He's been angling to stay with me here, but I…" She glanced down at her hands that had been plucking at the hem of her sweater. "I'm not ready to get married…or engaged. He's been pushing. He wasn't supposed to be here this week. We had an argument, and he said he was through with trying to get me to see reason. Said I didn't have to work. That he'd take care of me, but he didn't understand that this is my dream…"

"Didn't?" Victoria asked gently.

Harlie glanced up with eyes filled with tears. "He knows now. Said he will support me. Whatever I want to do. That's a big deal for him to say that. His family…is…powerful. I think they were the ones behind the kidnapping attempt in Costa Rica." She shook her head. "I was leaving the hotel to go to dinner with friends, and a car pulled up next to me. The next thing I knew, a man was trying to force me into the back seat. If two valets hadn't come to my rescue…" She blew out a breath. "His family… They have certain…prejudices…about American women, but especially actresses."

Victoria nodded. "Do you want to call him? Ask him to join us?"

Harlie took a deep breath. "Can we do this later? I'm hungry. And we have another party beside the pool. I don't want the person responsible to think they're getting to me. That I'm afraid. Can we tell him later?"

Victoria squeezed her hand. "Of course."

The actress cleared her throat. "So, what happens now?"

"We can keep monitoring the feed from our cameras. One of us will be at the party at all times. When you head back here, bring Adnan, and we'll talk."

"Two more days," Harlie said. "We've only got to get through two more days."

"And maybe more," Logan said, his gaze going

to Victoria. "Sadie needs to know that the problems could continue. Hank might want to assign more protectors to cover the set."

Harlie's head tilted to the side. And again, her expression changed. Her eyes sparkled a little as she stared back at them. "You know, I'm reading a script for a spy thriller. A married pair of spies. Maybe I could pick your brains about what it's like for the role. What she, my character, would know."

Relieved the woman was starting to relax, Victoria grinned. "Well, we're the folks to ask. I'm ex-FBI, and Logan here was a SEAL."

The woman's eyes rounded. "Real-life heroes." Her gaze went to Victoria and ran from her hair down to her toes. "Maybe I could model myself after you."

"Maybe."

Logan laughed. "Just make sure the hero's authentic. He should be constantly worried about what she's gonna do next. And he should do most of the rescuin'."

Victoria rolled her eyes. "He just needs to think he does."

LOGAN FOUND himself running through scenarios in his head while observing the group mingling poolside.

Tonight, to switch things up, Harlie had declared it a dress-up night. So, everyone had come wearing their shiniest, blingiest clothing.

He'd dressed in dark slacks, a button-up shirt, and a sports jacket. Victoria was wearing the black dress. The front was modest enough, covering all of her chest. The long sleeves were demure as well. It was the length that had him grinding his teeth. She wore no hosiery, and her slim legs gleamed from some shimmery cream she'd put on them. Every time she bent slightly over, he felt the urge to rush up behind her to make sure she didn't show her panties to the other men present.

Which wasn't something he'd ever felt the urge

to do with any other woman he'd dated. For some reason, he felt...possessive of her. He didn't like the way Trevor or Cal, or any of the cowboys serving drinks or carrying trays of canapes, looked at those long, toned legs. Those were *his* legs.

And then he caught himself and had to remind himself that she wasn't his. He'd had her once. They were partners. Working buddies. So, they'd had sex. He'd had sex plenty of times. Maybe she had, too.

And again, he felt something rise up in his chest. A tightness that no amount of breathing exercises would relieve.

So, he ran another scenario instead. Not his usual, with options for how to conclude a battle successfully. Rather, he considered options for how he'd make love to Victoria the next chance he got. If he ever got the chance again.

If Adnan decided to keep watch over Harlie tonight, he'd place the laptop with the feeds on the screen on the nightstand so that he could keep doing his job while he worshiped every inch of Victoria's body with his mouth and hands. Then he'd—

"So, you work with Sadie?"

Logan blinked, wondering how the hell Trevor had managed to come up next to him without him noticing. That had never happened before. "Yeah. I'm on her team," he answered.

"Someone mentioned you were out of the country before arriving here."

"I was."

Trevor snorted and nodded. "So, a new mystery project. Intriguing. Already casting?"

"Not yet. Still haven't nailed the story."

"Damn writers," Trevor muttered. "Probably won't finish the script until the actors arrive on the set anyway."

"That a problem for you? Learning lines on the fly?"

"Nah." Trevor tapped a finger against his temple. "Once I read it, it's there."

"That's a gift, man," Logan said, figuring now the man would turn the conversation to himself, and he could stop making shit up on the fly.

"That Harlie, she's something else," Trevor said, his gaze on the actress as she drew her assistant from her chair to dance.

Elaine was a mousy-looking woman whose mouse-brown hair always looked like it had been combed with her fingers. She didn't look at all pleased having everyone's eyes on her.

"Kind of reminds me of a mouse, ya know?"

Logan blinked again because hadn't he been thinking the exact same thing? "Harlie looks nothing like a mouse," he said, deliberately misinterpreting.

Trevor laughed. "I was talking about her

assistant. Dull brown hair, little pointy nose, long teeth."

"You're describing a rat."

Trevor laughed again and patted Logan's shoulder. Logan realized Trevor was swaying a little on his feet. "Really thought Meghan was going to get that part. We had great chemistry when we read together."

Logan turned his head to Trevor. "Who's Meghan?"

"My new girlfriend, Meghan Turner," he said, leering a bit. "Like I said. Great chemistry."

"So, someone else was considered for the part of the little sister?"

Trevor took a swallow from his wine glass. "Meghan was number one until Harlie read with Sadie. The executive producer—the *real* producer," he said, leaning toward Logan, "made his mind up on the spot."

Logan arched an eyebrow. "Real producer?"

"I've got nothing against Sadie or any other actor who likes to play at producing, but we all know that's a vanity title. Mug Leighton chose Harlie."

Logan had no idea who Mug Leighton was but figured he should nod sagely or Trevor might wonder why he didn't know who the "real" producer was. He also figured Sadie might be a little pissed having her role as producer dissed by this jackoff. "How did Meghan take getting passed over for the role?"

Trevor shuddered. "I didn't know a human could make sounds like that until she got the news she was on the outs. Kind of turned me on. You'll get a chance to meet her."

"Will she be visiting the set?"

"Looks like it. She's coming here tonight to see me." He glanced at his watch. "Should be arriving any minute. I arranged for a driver to pick her up at the airport."

"How long will she be staying?"

"Said she didn't have any other obligations, so she'll be coming with me when I report for work next week."

Logan glanced around to find Victoria. When he spotted her, his heart stilled.

"Scrape your tongue off the floor, man," Trevor said, and then gave a giggle that sounded decidedly feminine. "You struck the mother lode with that one."

Logan ignored the other man's wolf whistle and strode straight to the dance floor where Victoria had joined Harlie while they danced to Nelly's "Hot in Herre." Victoria danced stiffly while Harlie held back her blond hair and rubbed her belly against Victoria's backside. He almost laughed at his partner's reddening features. But damn, the women looked hot together. One dark-haired, one light.

One slender and lean, the other a voluptuous Barbie doll.

Everyone in the room seemed to note the contrasts, and Logan wanted to growl at the cowboys who couldn't keep their gazes off both women's bodies.

When he stopped in front of Victoria, she halted her weird-but-cute side-to-side swaying and pushed her long hair behind her ears.

Harlie gave a hoot and came to the side of the couple. "Are you going to ask her to dance, or did you want to join us?"

Everyone laughed, and Logan glared at Victoria, who was biting her lips to keep from grinning. He gave a deep sigh and held open his arms.

When she stepped into his arms, the song ended abruptly, replaced by something slow he thought might be sung by The Weeknd, but since that wasn't his kind of music, he wasn't sure. Worse, he found it hard to find the rhythm because of the fast and slow, off-beat track.

Victoria laughed then wrapped her arms low around his back, and "showed" him the beat. Soon, his hips moved with hers, which were dipping and rubbing—and basically driving him nuts. He bent toward her ear. "Why are you doing this?"

"Feels good, doesn't it?"

He rubbed his cheek against hers.

She shivered but said, "Ouch. You're going to give me whisker burn."

"Shut up. You like it."

They danced, barely moving their feet. Logan kept Harlie in his sight but concentrated on Victoria—how she felt sliding against him, how her ass felt beneath his palm.

Adnan moved behind Harlie and wrapped an arm around her waist. The pair fit perfectly together, dipping and bouncing softly. Every move mimicking sex. Others joined them in the crowded space between the loungers.

While holding Victoria's warm body, he fought to keep his attention on the others around him. For a second, he lost sight of Trevor but found him again when he led a redhead through the French doors. The woman's gaze swept the dancers then narrowed when she found Harlie.

Harlie gave the woman a beaming smile and a little wave but didn't move away from Adnan.

Logan assumed Trevor's girlfriend, the woman who had lost the part to Harlie, had just arrived. "Check out the woman with Trevor," he whispered in Victoria's ear.

"Who is she?" Victoria said, nuzzling his ear while angling her head toward the couple.

"She was supposed to get Harlie's part in the movie until Harlie read with Sadie."

"Look at you speaking all that film lingo," she teased. "Can I assume she didn't take it well?"

"Nope. She had a screamin' fit."

"She's all smiles now."

"She's an actress."

"You say that like it's a bad thing."

"I'm saying she can play a part. Hide her true feelings."

"So can we," she said, pulling back her head.

He remembered her years of undercover work and gave her a nod.

"So, the plot thickens, and now we have another suspect?" she whispered.

"Maybe. Not sure she'd have the power, or connections, to swing somethin' like this."

"Unless she didn't just arrive, and had an accomplice…"

He arched an eyebrow. "Like a cowboy she might've seduced or paid?"

She drew a deep breath then laid her cheek against his shoulder. "Maybe we're reaching. Getting paranoid."

"Occam's razor?" he murmured.

"Yeah, the simplest explanation…"

"What's simple about this though?"

"Adnan."

"Thought we'd ruled him out."

She tilted back her head, kissed his mouth, then said, "Maybe it's not him, but about him…?"

"Or maybe the problems on the set aren't related to those Harlie's been experiencin' here?"

Both her eyebrows rose. "Two suspects?"

"We really need to talk to Jake."

She nodded. "We should do it before we talk to Adnan."

"Agreed."

"So…?"

"We head back to the room, keep the live feed up so we have eyes on what's happening here, and make that call."

Victoria glanced toward Harlie. "I'll get with her and tell her not to go anywhere until one of us comes back down."

He gave her a nod. "See you upstairs." Then he gave her a kiss, so those around them could think what they liked about them disappearing upstairs alone. Then he turned her in his arms and gave her ass a pat, sending her toward Harlie.

Victoria let out a yelp and cast a mock-glare over her shoulder, but he wasn't worried about that look. She was smiling.

VICTORIA WATCHED Logan walk away with a smirk on his face. Lord, how she wished they were heading upstairs for a reason other than the fact they needed to talk with Jake about what else was going on here.

Harlie arched an eyebrow as she approached. Then she drew away from Adnan, glanced over her shoulder at him, and said, "Would you get me something to drink, babe?"

Adnan bowed his head and departed.

Harlie wrapped her arms around Victoria. "Saw your SEAL leaving," she whispered.

"We're calling our team. We've got lots of leads they need to look into so we can figure out who is doing this."

"We still on to bring Adnan into the conversation?" she asked.

"I think it would be wisest. We can't be with you 24/7 without folks wondering what's going on and alerting whoever is behind these attacks that we're not who we said we were. We'd feel better if he kept close."

"He'll like that," she said with a waggle of her eyebrows.

Victoria gave her a pointed look. "While we're gone, don't leave this patio. We'll be watching."

She wrinkled her nose. "I'm still a little wigged out about all those cameras."

"Better that than the alternative…"

"I guess." She sighed then gave a blazing smile.

Victoria glanced back to see Adnan approaching, holding a glass of wine. "That's my cue," she muttered.

"Later," Harlie said, already reaching for the

glass as Adnan stepped closer and encircled her waist to bring her body close.

Victoria left them dancing, passing Cal and Pauline, who were seated on loungers and drinking beers. When she passed Trevor, he was dancing with Meghan, their heads close as they talked. She noted how his gaze swept the other dancers. Not exactly a man who was making his partner the focus of his attention, but if you were talking about something you didn't want overheard…

She shook her head as she swept through the French doors. Definitely paranoid. She couldn't wait until they could figure out who was trying to hurt Harlie, because all this second-guessing was getting old.

CHAPTER 13

WHEN SHE ARRIVED BACK at the room, Logan was already seated in the armchair, his cell phone to his ear. He beckoned her over with a wave of his hand.

"She just walked in. I'll put the call on speaker."

Feeling a little frisky, she strode toward him, but rather than taking the chair opposite his, she settled onto his thigh and wrapped her arm around his shoulders to snuggle closer.

His gaze narrowed, but he laid his free hand on her thigh.

"Evening, Jake," she said.

"Beck's here, too, along with Cygny."

"Hi, girls," she said, smiling. She did miss her friends.

"So, Logan said you have an update, but let me talk about what Swede dug up on Anita Harris first," Jake said. "Anita's record is as clean as a whistle. She lives with her mother, who has early-onset dementia. She mortgaged her house a few months ago to pay for in-home health care for when she has to work."

"So, she's vulnerable to a bribe," Logan murmured.

"And she may have taken one. She hasn't touched her checking account in over two weeks, which is unusual for her because her bank history shows she uses her debit card for big and small purchases, sometimes several times a day."

"So, she was probably paid in cash," Victoria said.

"Looks like it."

"She's pretty much off social media, except for a Facebook account where she's active in gardening and dementia groups. No apparent connections to your celebrities."

"I don't think we should corner her and ask her about the camera just yet. I don't want her acting *squirrely*," she said, wrinkling her nose at Logan. "She might tip off whoever paid her that we know what she did."

"They likely know there was an issue but might put it down to her not installing it correctly," Logan said.

"All right, that's all we have," Jake said. "What's been happening? We already know about the ATV brake line being cut."

"Earlier, the girth strap for her saddle was sawed through," Logan said. "She slid off with the saddle in the middle of a ride."

"She's okay?"

"Yeah. A bit banged up and worried about what Sadie will think about the bruises and scrapes, but she's fine."

"Good," Jake said. "Any clues yet who might be behind this?"

"We've got a list…" Victoria said.

"Give it to me. I'll have Swede do background checks and look at their financials."

"We had Adnan at the top of our list," Logan began, "but he looked completely shocked both times she was threatened. He's also showing signs he's not leaning on her as much about her work."

"He's completely pie-eyed," Victoria added.

"Pie-eyed?" Beck said then snickered.

Logan's nose wrinkled as well at the term.

"You know," she said, looking directly into Logan's eyes and leaning toward him, her lips hovering over his, "long soulful looks, ready to jump in to see to her comfort. There when she needs him."

Logan swallowed hard, and his hand tightened on her thigh.

"So, the man's in love, huh?" her friend said.

"That's my opinion," she said, smirking as she glanced at the phone again. "I don't think he's good for any of this. However, do we know how happy or unhappy his family might be about him falling for an American actress? Harlie mentioned they have prejudices about American women, so her being an actress might put her completely beyond the pale."

"On it," Jake said. "I'll see if Swede can broaden the search around Adnan; see if anyone in the family, or their employees, has been in Wyoming lately."

Logan cleared his throat. "Then there's Cal and Pauline…"

"Cal's the cameraman, and Pauline's Harlie's makeup artist," Beck said softly, as though she was reviewing the players in a folder.

"Yeah, there's just something about them," Logan said. "Something shifty."

"And that camera rail failed… Cal would've had the knowledge and the opportunity to rig it to fail. I'll add him to the list," Jake said.

"I've got no clue why either of them would want to sink the movie," Victoria said, shaking her head. "I don't see the motive."

"Now, we can add Trevor Hanson, her co-star," Logan said. "He told me there was another actress, Meghan Turner, who was top of the list for Harlie's part, but that Harlie got it after she read with Sadie. The executive producer, Mug Leighton, made that decision. Now, Trevor has invited Meghan, who appears to be his girlfriend at the moment, to the ranch."

"So, you think they could be sabotaging Harlie so his girlfriend can step in to replace her when she gets hurt?" Cygny asked.

"Can't rule the pair of them out," Logan muttered. "Both appear to be sharks."

"And there's one more thing," Victoria said.

"Want to add someone else to the list?"

"Nope." She blew out a breath. "We've told Harlie why we're here."

There was a pause, then, "Good call," Jake said. "She's in danger. If she'll think twice about putting herself in the crosshairs, it's a good thing."

"She wants to tell Adnan. And Logan and I agree that would be a good decision. We can't cover her when she's in her suite—not without letting whoever is behind this know we're not who we say we are."

"You trust him?"

Victoria met Jake's gaze, and he nodded.

"We do," he said.

"All right. Just so you know, Beck and her teammate, Roman, have a bit of a break right now. They're going to Jackson Hole. Figure out Harlie's plans and how they can integrate without raising any red flags."

"Will do," Logan said.

"Out here."

The call ended, and Logan's head turned toward her. "You know what you're sitting on, don't you?"

How could she have missed it? She arched an eyebrow. "Can't be comfortable," she said, wiggling her bottom on his thigh and the telltale bulge running parallel to it.

Both their gazes went to the feeds on the patio. Harlie's party was still in full swing. Adnan was by her side, his arm encircling her lower back as they talked to Trevor and Meghan.

Logan groaned.

Victoria laughed softly. "After we have a chat with him, Adnan will stay with her tonight. I doubt he'll let her pee without watching her."

"We can keep the laptop on the nightstand, so we can continue to watch the feeds."

She turned inward, toward him and looped her other arm around his shoulders. "We could multi-task. Aren't SEALs masters at multi-tasking?"

Logan's hands went to her ass, and he lifted her, waiting as she slipped one leg over his lap so she could straddle him. The hem of her dress slipped to mid-bottom, and his hands took advantage, cupping both cheeks.

"You wore a goddamn thong?" he muttered.

"Would you rather I had gone without any underwear at all? This dress would've shown every panty line."

He shook his head, and his fingers gripped her

tighter. "I spent the evening grittin' my teeth every time you looked like you were gonna bend over."

"Harlie shows just as much of her ass when she's in a bikini."

"Harlie's ass isn't mine."

Victoria blinked.

Logan quickly looked away.

She didn't know whether she was pleased or uneasy that he felt possessive of her ass. Still, she wasn't about to pick apart his words just now when something more interesting was happening beneath her spread legs.

"Roll like that again, and I'll consider it an invitation," he growled.

"I didn't roll," she lied. "I…shifted, seeing as how my *seat* is getting lumpy."

His lips rolled between his teeth, forming a straight line. "That's not a lump."

She loosely wrapped her arms around his shoulders and rubbed her breasts against his chest. "And these aren't pointy because they're cold."

Logan's face screwed up into a ferocious scowl. "You do pick your moments."

"We could be quick," she whispered and gave a little bounce which had him sucking in his breath.

Logan's hands left her ass, and his fingers sank into her hair, bringing her face to his. His kiss was hard and thorough. His dick pulsed between them.

When they both parted to drag in air, he

cupped her bottom again and stood. Just as she was getting ready to wrap her legs around his hips, he slapped a bare cheek then slowly set her on her feet.

Her hands clutched his shoulders, but only long enough for the swaying to end.

He tapped the end of her nose. "After we get Adnan briefed up, we'll continue this conversation."

She slowly pushed her dress down to cover her assets. "I hope I don't drop anything," she said then walked toward the door, knowing his gaze was following the wag of her hips.

BACK AT THE PARTY, Logan stood next to the bar with a hand in his pocket to mask the slight tenting that no amount of internal cajoling could ease. He found his attention constantly wandering from Harlie and Adnan back to his partner, who always seemed to manage to be facing away from him, the hem of her skirt rising dangerously high every time she flicked her hair behind her shoulder. She was teasing him. And it was working.

Lord have mercy, she was a sight to behold. He'd always thought he preferred blondes, but Victoria's dark brunette hair was a lovely contrast to her golden skin. Her eyes were his favorite feature, their color like a warm, dark whisky, and her dark-winged brows were so expressive he could read her thoughts by whether they lowered or how they arched. Her plump lips…

Damn, he adjusted himself again. No use going there, not when they still had work to do.

At last, Harlie and Adnan bid their guests farewell and made their way back into the house.

Victoria left a minute later, snagging a glass of wine to take with her and laughing at something Trevor said as she passed him and Meghan.

Logan left right after her, catching up to her at the bottom of the staircase. Together, they climbed the steps and made their way to Harlie's room.

Victoria tapped on the door. Logan glanced back down the hallway to see whether anyone was around, but there was no one when Harlie opened the door to the suite. They quickly entered and approached a confused-looking Adnan, who raised an inquiring eyebrow at his girlfriend.

Logan held up a finger to his lips then signaled to Victoria to begin a search of the room. Together, they made sure there were no new listening devices or cameras and returned to the sitting room. Logan gave Harlie a nod, telling her silently that she could begin this little chat.

"They aren't with the film crew," Harlie said. "They're my protection detail."

Adnan's head drew back, and then he looked closer at Logan and Victoria. "Is this about the accidents? What's going on?"

"Neither incident was an accident," Victoria said, taking the seat Harlie indicated while the actress sat next to Adnan on the loveseat and Logan lowered into another armchair.

Together, he and Victoria described what had happened at the ranch and at the film's set. When they finished, Adnan's face was tight and angry.

"A camera was installed in this room?"

Logan nodded. "Do you have any idea who might be interested to know who Harlie sleeps with?"

Adnan leaned back and ran a hand over his face. When his gaze met Harlie's there was sorrow in his eyes. "My family might be responsible for some of this. They weren't happy when I refused to return home."

"They asked you to go back to Saudi Arabia?" she said, her eyes widening.

He nodded. "They want me to marry. They have the girl already chosen. Her father is a general in the Royal Saudi Armed Forces."

Harlie moved to the corner of the sofa. "Why didn't you tell me?"

"Because it is nothing to do with us," he said. "I have told them I'm not interested." He waved a hand. "They are cutting me off. Disowning me. I told them it wouldn't change anything. My life is here," he said, his gaze pleading with Harlie's. "I have been working toward ending my affiliation with my family for a couple of years now—separating my US businesses from theirs. I already hold dual passports. I can surrender my Saudi passport and live fully as an American."

"I didn't know things were that bad with your family."

"I didn't want you to. They are poisonous. In bed with other vipers. I didn't want any of that to touch you."

Harlie drew a deep breath then reached out a hand to him. He held it and raised it to his lips.

Logan leaned forward in his chair. "Do you think they could've been behind the attacks on Harlie?"

He shrugged. "This general who wanted me to be his son-in-law could've organized a hit squad. He has the resources and the cunning. He's absolutely ruthless. It could be."

Victoria frowned. "What about the things that happened on the set?"

Adnan shook his head. "I don't think they would've had any interest in the movie. They would only be focused on ending my relationship with Harlie."

Logan glanced at Victoria. "So, we're back to two separate entities."

Adnan placed a hand over his heart. "I thank you both for being here and seeing to her safety."

"It's our job and our pleasure, but we're gonna need your help going forward," Logan said.

Adnan gave a quick, curt nod. "Of course. Whatever Harlie needs."

"Keep in mind, whoever is responsible can't know why we're here. We'll need you to stick close to Harlie whenever we aren't around, and you both need to use some situational awareness—pay attention to what's happenin' around you and keep your doors locked. I'd even put a chair against the door when we leave in case someone tries to come through it, although, so far, they haven't made any open attacks. They've tried to make things look like accidents."

Adnan straightened in his chair. "I will stay close to Harlie. I would give my life for her."

Harlie's eyes glistened. "That's the hottest thing you've ever said."

Logan pressed his lips together to keep from laughing.

"Give me your phones," Victoria said. "I'll put our numbers in them so you can call us directly if anything happens or even if you're not sure you're in trouble. Better to be safe than sorry."

They turned over their phones to her, and she stored their cellphone numbers and returned them.

"What's on tomorrow's events calendar?" Logan asked.

Adnan frowned and looked at Harlie. "You should stay here."

Harlie's eyebrows lowered. "If we don't follow through with our plans, whoever is doing this will know we're onto them." She turned to Logan and Victoria. "Tomorrow, we're supposed to hike to Delta Lake in Grand Teton National Park. It's a day hike. A little strenuous."

Logan nodded. "We'll be with you. No need to change your plans. We'll ride together to and from the trailhead." He pushed up from his seat and reached out to shake Adnan's hand. "Call if you hear so much as a floorboard squeak."

After they left the couple, Logan took Victoria's hand. They started at a sedate pace down the hall-way, but then their steps sped up. By the time they reached the stairs, they were running.

CHAPTER 14

THEY ARRIVED breathless at their door.

Victoria giggled then pressed her fingers against her lips because the sound wasn't one she usually made, and it embarrassed her. Logan used his key to open the door and swept a hand inside, inviting her to precede him.

She gave him a quick glance and read the lust in the heightened color of his cheeks and the glinting silver of his eyes. Any embarrassment fled with her surging confidence. He wanted her. She'd put that look on his face.

She strode past him, walking into their room then glanced back over her shoulder to watch him move toward her.

Logan placed the key on the desk and unbuttoned the cuffs of his shirt. "Did you know you nearly showed your ass every time you raised your hand to flip your hair?"

She turned to face him and pouted her mouth, nearly ruining the gesture when his narrowing gaze made her lips twitch. "No one would've raised an eyebrow. They're used to baring skin."

He shook his head as he moved toward her. "You make me feel things I shouldn't."

She raised her chin and her eyebrows. "Like?"

"Like the sight of your ass shouldn't be anyone else's to enjoy."

She shivered at the way his voice deepened into a rasping growl. "But I didn't let anyone else see it."

"I didn't want anyone else even anticipatin' that pleasure."

"Sounds like your problem, not mine."

"Do you like playin' with fire?"

She found that she did. Taking a step closer, she reached out and slid her palm over the front of his pants. "I see your problem now," she whispered then licked her lips as she stared up at him.

He lowered his head and touched his mouth to hers in the barest of caresses. "It's been like that all night. And it's all your doin'."

Her smile was quick, and then she rose upward to rub her mouth on his with a little more pressure than he'd applied. She sucked on his lower lip before she leaned her head away.

His nostrils flared, and his eyelids dipped halfway.

When she would have moved straight into his arms, he cupped her shoulders, holding her away. Before she could muster a complaint, he sank to his knees in front of her.

"Hold up your skirt," he said, his voice sounding hoarse.

Not the place she'd thought he'd begin. *Oh my.*

Trembling, she slid her hands down her hips then clenched the fabric to slowly raise the hem, not stopping until she'd lifted it above her panties.

"I've been dreamin' about this all night," he said, tracing the lacy elastic straps that encircled her hips with his fingers and then his tongue.

She inched her feet apart to give him access.

When he stroked his tongue over the small triangle covering her sex, her knees nearly buckled. She dropped a hand onto the top of his head to steady herself as he slid his fingers beneath the elastic and slowly dragged her panties downward.

When his tongue touched her heated flesh directly, she found she couldn't suck in a deep enough breath. She gave a tiny whimper when he flicked his tongue over her clit. He followed with teasing glides between her folds and flutters against her clit that she soon found frustrating.

Victoria sank her fingers into his hair and tugged.

He kissed the top of her thigh and glanced upward, a wicked half-smile on his lips.

"You're driving me crazy," she said, giving him a glare.

"Then we're even." He pushed up from the floor, tucked fingers beneath one breast and bent to kiss the tip through the fabric. "These pants are about to become a problem," he said, his nose scrunching.

She couldn't help laughing. "Glad I'm not the only one frustrated as hell." She dropped the hem of her skirt and slid around him, heading toward the bed. "You coming?" she said, giving him a flirtatious glance over her shoulder.

As he strode toward her, he opened his belt and slowly drew it from the loops.

Victoria raised a finger and wagged it at him. "No more stalling. I've been as horny as you all night."

She raised her skirt, sat on the edge of the bed, then scooted backward up the mattress, keeping her legs parted just enough to give him teasing glimpses of her sex.

Logan unbuttoned two buttons at the top of his shirt then quickly dragged it over his head. He kicked off his shoes, dug into his pocket for his wallet, which he tossed onto the bed, then shoved down his pants. Then he climbed onto the mattress, stalking her to where she was sitting, her back against the headboard and still wearing the dress but with her bottom half exposed.

His gaze dropped to the dress. "Feel like indulgin' a fantasy?"

Her mouth stretched slowly into a smile. "Does it call for you to don a condom anytime soon?"

He reached sideways for his wallet. "As a matter of fact…"

Victoria watched as he applied a condom. Then he knelt next to her and pointed to a spot on the bed in front of him. "I want you here."

When she started to crawl toward him, he twirled a finger. Understanding immediately, she turned around and knelt, waiting for him to come up behind her.

"That skirt… You teased me all night long. I imagined you bendin' to pick something up, and I had to fight myself not to jump behind you to keep you from showin' your—"

"Assets?" she said smiling as he pushed her hair from her neck and nuzzled behind her ear.

"Yeah. That's for my eyes only."

She shivered when he sucked at the skin on her neck, knowing he'd leave a hickey, but not really caring.

His hands smoothed over her breasts, lifting them and squeezing. Then he smoothed over her belly and sides, and down between her legs, rubbing the fabric of her dress against her pussy.

Victoria reached an arm behind her and clutched the back of his head while grinding her bottom against him.

His hands moved again, this time to clutch her skirt and slowly lift it. Then he moved back and pressed between her shoulder blades until she leaned over and braced herself against the mattress.

"Yeah, that's the view I imagined," he said, his fingertips trailing over her skin, on either side of her ass. Then one hand cupped her between her legs.

Her back sank, lifting her bottom.

Fingers traced her folds then slipped inside.

She backed onto them then pulled away, and then surged backward again, trying to tempt him into giving her something more substantial than his fingers. When his thumb began rubbing her clit, she hissed between gritted teeth because it felt so damn good. She'd wanted this—him—all evening long. Teasing him while they'd taken the call had been a tactical blunder on her part because she'd been hyper-aware of him the entire night.

One thought she refused to let root and grow was that she'd never felt this intense of a reaction to a man before. He was all wrong for her. He thought he should protect her, that she was the weaker sex and needed his protection. Plus, he was her partner, and hadn't she promised herself to never, ever let herself get too involved with someone she might lose on the job? He was a distraction. Tonight had proven that point.

Still, she needed what he was about to give her like she needed sustenance. Her body was primed, her breaths broken and shallow, her center melting around his fingers.

"Logan…"

"I'm right here with you, babe."

His fingers withdrew, he shifted on the bed behind her, and then she felt him nudge against her opening. Fisting her hands in the bedding beneath her, she braced, holding still as he slowly pushed inside her and then bent over her back, his face snuggling into the corner of her neck as he began to move. His hands glided down her arms, and his fingers intertwined with hers.

"Fuck, you're so hot," he whispered as his hips began to move in more powerful glides.

She squeezed her inner muscles around him and began to pump backward, meeting his thrusts. Logan reared backward, and gripped the notches of her hips, pulling her into his thrusts, pushing her away as he withdrew, controlling their movements. He powered into her, forcing air out of her lungs in sharp gusts, but she loved it. She tossed back her hair and dropped her chest to the mattress, frustrated that her dress prevented her from rubbing her chest against the coverlet.

He came at her, harder and harder, and she

began to moan and mew, needing more as she approached the zenith.

"Touch yourself," he gritted out.

She slid a hand down her belly and into the top of her folds, found her clit, and began to rub it. "*Yesss*," she hissed. "Jesus, Logan!"

The moment her pleasure exploded, he gave her three short, sharp thrusts and held still inside her—but only for a moment. She felt the pulse of his eruption before he moved again, his strokes slowing, lengthening. He somehow managed to keep her at the peak, and she reveled in the slow unwinding of the coiled tension in her belly.

When she slumped against the mattress, spent, he moved his legs outside of hers and followed her downward, covering her back. He pressed kisses along her shoulder, and she turned her head. His mouth grazed the side of hers.

"Holy shit," he whispered. He expelled a deep breath and then rolled away. "I'll get the laptop."

She blinked. Reality intruded, arresting her moment of bliss. She rolled to her back and stared at the ceiling. With a shake of her head to clear it, she said, "Would you roll back the recordings?"

"On it," he said.

She glanced at him, leaning over the desk, his back to her. She admired the muscles still gleaming with sweat. She'd had that well-muscled, powerful body. Her lips pursed as she blew out a stream of air.

Shaking her head again, she dragged her glance away. He was a distraction all right. A big, two-hundred-pound mass of honed muscle and testosterone. Lord, he fucked like a god.

Victoria swung her legs over the side of the bed and pushed off the mattress. "I'm going to shower."

He nodded but didn't glance back. His gaze was on the laptop, his talented fingers tapping to scroll through the feeds. His mind was already on the job.

Must be nice to have that kind of focus.

Hers was shot. Blown away. Feeling a little dismayed, she padded to the bathroom. She might have to request a new partner when she got back to Colorado because she couldn't keep her mind on the job. Someone was going to get hurt…or worse.

LOGAN WAITED until the bathroom door closed then let out a deep breath. He settled on the chair in front of the desk and glared down at his dick. He quickly removed the condom, tied it, and tossed it into the trashcan beside the desk.

He still couldn't believe they'd forgotten to set the laptop up on the nightstand as they'd planned. Although all was quiet, and he'd detected no problems when rolling back the feed, the opportunity for disaster had been there. He'd been so focused on getting Victoria into bed that he'd completely forgotten the mission. That had never happened to him before.

Then again, he'd never had a female partner. Maybe this assignment to the Athena Project wasn't such a good idea. At least not for him. However, he didn't like the idea of requesting reassignment because then he wouldn't be around to have Victoria's six.

He wouldn't trust another man to be as careful and mindful of the fact that, while she was in great shape and well-trained, she was still a woman. Something he couldn't quite get his thick Neanderthal head around.

Yeah, he knew he was sexist. Knew this was his issue, not hers. The thought of her being out on a dangerous mission without him to cover her killed him. No, he'd stick it out, but he'd have to do something to try to compartmentalize his attraction. Tamp it down. When he was on the job, he'd maintain mission focus. Only afterward would he let his mind wander down more pleasurable paths.

He wondered if he explained it that way to her whether she'd be on board.

The sound of the shower starting drew his attention, and he imagined her standing nude under the spray, lather falling in bubbly ropes over her proud, uptilted breasts…

Logan sighed and picked up the laptop. He took

it to Victoria's nightstand and set it there. The second she was out of the shower, he'd head inside and take care of the issue rising between his legs, again.

As much as he wanted to make love to her all night long, they had a job to do, a young woman to protect. Mission first. When this was all over, they might have to sit down for a long chat about how things with them should go.

Relief poured over him. They were both adults. They'd find a way to work together going forward. A part of him hoped she wouldn't be too agreeable. That she'd feel at least a little disappointment over his decision.

The bathroom door opened, and he strode to the closet to retrieve his toiletry bag.

Victoria stepped into the room surrounded by a cloud of steam, a towel wrapped around her slim body.

Her gaze swept his nude frame, and he nearly smirked because it snagged on his dick. He couldn't help the little surge of male pride that she seemed to like what she was seeing.

She blinked. When she looked up at his face, her expression was a little wary. "It's all yours." Then she quickly bit her bottom lip.

His glance swept over her head to toe. "Yeah, it is," he quipped, and he couldn't help that his voice sounded a little hoarse.

She raised a finger to point over her shoulder. "The shower. I meant, the shower."

He grinned as he passed her. "Sure you did."

"Asshole," she whispered.

So, they definitely weren't going for round two, but she had checked him out.

CHAPTER 15

THE GROUP MAKING the trek to Delta Lake was dropped at the trailhead the following morning, along with their gear, all of which had been provided by the ranch.

Victoria checked her backpack and saw that it was filled with water bottles and bagged sandwiches, an apple, and wipes. Beside her pack lay a set of trekking poles. "Are we really going to need those?" she asked, looking toward Harlie.

Harlie shrugged. "I haven't hiked this trail, but I hear it can be rugged in places. Better safe than sorry."

"Who is this woman?" Adnan quipped, holding a hand against his heart, his eyebrows raised.

Harlie gave one of her tinkling laughs. "I don't go skydiving without a parachute."

He shuddered. "I'll take trekking poles over parachutes any day."

Cal walked by and gave a smile that looked like more of a grimace. "I read that this hike is just over eight miles. I'm glad Pauline skipped it. She'd have complained the whole way."

"Are you sure you want to do it?" Harlie asked. "It starts out pretty easy, but we'll be climbing after a bit. And the terrain does get pretty rocky."

Cal hesitated for a moment then drew a deep breath. "Smell that air? I wouldn't miss this."

Elaine, Harlie's assistant, stopped beside him. "Sure beats LA smog." Still, she looked a little daunted as she stared down the trail.

"I'm surprised neither Trevor or Meghan joined us today," Logan murmured, lifting an eyebrow.

Harlie snorted. "They're both afraid of scrapes and fractures. Have to keep their bodies film-set ready."

So, she too suspected that Meghan had an ulterior motive for sticking close to the production.

Victoria pushed up and slipped her arms through the straps of the backpack. Then she placed her hands inside the straps on the trekking poles and clutched them. "I've never used these. If they get annoying, I'll just tie them to my pack."

Logan reached out his pole and tapped her ass. "Are we a little grumpy this morning?"

"We're feeling just fine," she replied with a narrowed glance.

"One more chance, folks," Harlie called out. "The last vehicle can take you back if you're not sure this is for you."

"Wouldn't miss it," another of Harlie's entourage called out.

Victoria arched an eyebrow at Logan, who gave her a smile. This little hike would be a piece of cake for both of them. They'd relayed their destination to Beck and Roman and knew they'd be seeing them somewhere along the trail, or perhaps when they returned to the trailhead. They'd figure out a way to make their integration into the group seem a natural happenstance. Having backup for the rest of this little job would certainly be welcome. Although, now that they wouldn't have to be watching their target 24/7, how would they use their free time?

She knew it wasn't wise, but hoped she'd be spending a little more alone time with Logan. A thought that gave her pause. He was consuming way too much of her thoughts, although looking at him now, she conceded it was only natural. Everything about him appealed to her—his well-honed physique, his sharp mind, and eye for trouble. She was also beginning to like his masculine courtesies, like letting her precede him through a door or onto a trail, or seeing to little comforts, like bringing her drinks or as he'd done this morning at breakfast—tucking her hair behind her ear to keep it out of her plate. She'd sighed when he'd done that, and then stared at his mouth because she'd wanted a kiss.

And when he'd obliged her, she'd melted into a puddle of goo.

She was going soft on him. She really, really liked him. Her stomach was a nervous blend of hope and dread because she was pretty sure she was falling for him.

Today was going to be a problem. Beck knew her all too well. She'd read the signs that something was going on between her and her new partner. Beck wouldn't have a problem with that, but she would have a good laugh. She knew all too well that she and Logan had rubbed each other the wrong way when they'd first been paired. This new development would have her laughing her ass off.

In the meantime, they had a little hike to get through. With no engines or saddles to sabotage, she hoped the trip to the alpine lake would be unexciting. Plus, she needed the exercise. After days of light activity, she was looking forward to pushing herself a bit. Stretched, sore muscles might take her mind off the man standing beside her.

Naturally, Harlie took the lead after referring to her map of the trail. Victoria no longer thought that Harlie did this to make sure everyone knew who was the center of attention here. Harlie wasn't a narcissist—she was everyone's cheerleader, determined to keep everyone's spirits high. She set the example, setting out with a smile and a twinkle of excitement in her eyes.

Poor, besotted Adnan was there to lend support if she needed it. To protect her back, if she would let him. Victoria found his devotion sweet and hoped Harlie didn't break the man's heart. He strode beside her until they reached a narrow wooden bridge.

Everyone ahead and behind Victoria chattered good-naturedly as they walked. Beyond the narrow walking bridge, the path grew rocky with small stones littering the trail and larger ones jutting out in places.

The poles were actually helpful when the ground wasn't even, so she wasn't quite ready to pitch them into the woods.

"Do much hiking?" Logan asked as he came up beside her.

"Not since college. I ran trails in Virginia, but nothing like this," she said, eyeing the tall peaks in the distance.

"We don't have mountains like this in Oklahoma either, but we've got some rugged country. It can be challengin', too."

"I'd think after all the time you spent carrying a heavy pack in the SEALs this would be the last thing you'd want to do for fun."

"I've missed our workouts," he said, waggling his eyebrows. "I'm starting to lose muscle tone."

She laughed. "Yeah, throwing me around on a mat has to be exhausting."

He threw back his head and gave a long groan. "You still holdin' that against me?"

"Nope, but I think I need to pick another SEAL's brain for a way to even up my chances."

"Think any of the guys will give away our secrets?"

With a smug smile, she lifted her chin. "I'm sure one of them would love to see you land on your ass for a change."

About a mile and a half in, the dirt trail narrowed until hikers had to continue in a single file. There wasn't much conversation because they were climbing. Although she was in good shape, she was now glad of the trekking poles, which she used to grip the dirt in front of her as she moved. Rock outcroppings made it so she had to keep her gaze on the ground rather than on the amazing scenery.

She nearly ran into Adnan's back when he came to an unannounced halt.

Ahead, Harlie stood on a small atoll, holding out her arms and turning slowly. "Can you believe this view?"

They were above most of the trees now, and the hills were topped with thick grass and—surprise,

surprise—more rocks. Snuggled in a valley below them was a small lake, surrounded by lush forest.

Harlie pulled the map out of her back pocket. "That's not our destination, so cool your jets. The trail's gonna get worse up ahead."

"Worse?" Cal said, wiping the back of his hand across his sweaty brow.

Harlie jogged her eyebrows up and down. "You're not quitting on me, are you?"

Cal wrinkled his nose. "No, ma'am."

"The trail is going to give way to a couple of rocky fields. You'll need to step on the larger stones because the smaller ones can shift, and we don't want anyone breaking an ankle. Take your time when we get there."

She set off again, and her pace didn't really slow despite the steep climb. Soon, they arrived at the first of the rocky fields.

"I don't see a trail," Elaine said, her face red and her breaths puffing.

Harlie pointed with her pole up the side of the field. "No marked trail, too many rocks, but we're going up. Choose your steps wisely."

Elaine shifted her pack and tightened her mouth, but when Harlie charged forward, she followed.

Logan and Victoria hung back.

"Might be a good idea to follow the group in case anyone gets into trouble," Logan murmured.

"Yeah, I was thinking the same thing. Elaine's not in any kind of shape for this."

"Cal was struggling, too."

They shared a glance. "Trying to keep up with a twenty-something girl isn't easy."

Everyone made it up the rocky hillside.

Elaine groaned when they found the trail on the other side. It was downhill for about a minute, and then they encountered the second rocky hillside.

"For fuck's sake," Cal said softly.

Ahead, Harlie laughed. "The reward is just beyond this hill. Promise!"

When they reached the top, everyone paused, phones came out, and many selfies followed. A jewel of a lake stretched before them.

"Don't stop now!" Harlie called out then started to work her way sideways down a dirt wash that ended at the edge of Delta Lake. Trees surrounded the deep blue water that looked slightly cloudy.

"Lord, I can't wait to swim," Elaine said.

Logan grinned. "You might dip your toes in first. I'll bet it's icicle-cold."

Victoria didn't care how cold it was. She couldn't wait to rest her feet in the water and wash some of the trail dust off her face. And eat.

They didn't have the lake to themselves. A few other hikers were already claiming boulders next to the water to rest on.

One particular couple looked familiar.

Beck and her partner Roman glanced at Harlie's group and waved.

"The view is spectacular," Beck called out.

Harlie smiled and tilted her head. She must have noted the nod Roman gave Logan. "Friends of yours?" she asked when she came up beside Victoria.

"Yup. Our backup," she whispered. "Come meet them."

"The Protectors certainly have a type," she said, her tone wry.

Victoria saw her point. Roman and Logan both sported short-cropped, dark hair and well-muscled bodies. Beck was curvier than Victoria, but her well-toned legs proved her high level of fitness. As well, she was brown-haired and brown-eyed, although her eyes had flecks of gold.

Victoria waved Adnan over. "Harlie, Adnan, meet Beck Morrissey and Roman McClain. They're friends of ours," she said, emphasizing *friends* in case anyone overheard. "Beck, Roman… Meet Harlie James and Adnan Khan. Harlie's been hosting a house party at a nearby ranch."

Adnan reached out to shake their hands. "I'm very happy to meet you," he said solemnly.

"We're going to eat lunch and head back. Care to join us?" Harlie said loudly enough that others in her group could hear. Then she winked.

"We'd love the company," Beck said, smiling. "So, how was that climb?"

While the two women walked away, Victoria took advantage of the cool water to wash up, and then took off her hiking boots and socks and stepped into the water. "Wow, that's cold!" she said, grimacing.

"I did warn you," Logan said.

She hurried out of the water and sat on a nearby boulder, laying her boots and socks beside her. "It was worth it. I should've broken in the boots a bit before making such a long hike."

Logan lifted each of her feet and inspected them. "You're working on a blister here," he said, lifting one foot high enough she had to brace herself on her hands or rock backward.

"A little warning?" she said with a slight glare.

"I have something for that," he said, ignoring her look, and dropped his pack beside the boulder and rooted through it for his first aid kit. "This plaster should do the trick."

After he cut a piece and applied it to her heel, then washed up in the lake, he pulled out a sandwich and a bag of chips. "Problems feel like they're a world away up here, don't they?"

"It is beautiful. Peaceful," she agreed, taking a bite of her ham and Swiss cheese sandwich. "Lord, this tastes good," she said around a full mouth, glancing around to make sure their target was safe.

Harlie and Adnan found a large boulder and invited Beck and Roman to sit with them.

Logan's gaze went to the trees around them. "Great spot for a sniper."

"Good thing our bad guys prefer keeping their op on the down-low."

"And they would've had to use the same trail to get here. I doubt they're mountaineers, too."

Victoria tipped her chin toward Cal and Elaine, who sat next to each other. "Wonder what they're talking about."

"Cal's the only one with his lips moving."

"Which means he's probably griping about the hike."

"Elaine looks too worn out to waste energy on talking."

They shared a grin until she realized they were staring at each other, maybe a little too long. She glanced toward Beck, who was smirking back at her, and she guessed Beck had reached all the right conclusions about what she and Logan had been up to since they'd arrived in Jackson Hole.

"We should probably talk..." Logan began.

"Or not," she said, feeling an instant tension form between her shoulders. All her internal arguments came screaming back at her.

"We'll have to at some point," he said, spearing her with a look.

"I'm thinking about asking for a reassignment," she blurted, and then instantly wished she hadn't.

"Wow. Not what I expected." His eyebrows lowered, and he glanced toward the lake. "What about us?"

"I don't think 'us' is a good idea," she said softly.

He grunted and dropped the hand holding what remained of his sandwich, like he didn't find it appealing any more. "When did you decide this?"

She shrugged, feeling...wrong. Like she was being mean or cruel, but how could they continue to work together when neither of them could keep their attention on the job at hand. Once she was reassigned, they'd be constantly having to work around schedules that would never synch up, and she wasn't into quickies. She wouldn't be satisfied with a quick "Logan fix" every now and then.

No, she wanted all of him. All the time. Which just wouldn't work.

This is for the best, she told herself, and while her internal argument was logical, she still felt...awful.

She straightened her shoulders. "Look, you're great. I mean, I like you." Only that word felt very inadequate for what she felt for him. He was a good guy. A bit old-fashioned in his views, but a natural protector. Strong, brave, honest. All qualities she admired and would want in a life partner.

If that was what she was looking for. But she wasn't ready to settle down. She still had years of doing this kind of work—work she found rewarding and exciting. Why should she settle for less? He certainly wouldn't.

Logan stayed silent for a long moment then pushed up from the rock, wrapped up the remains of his sandwich, and strode toward the group around Harlie, leaving Victoria feeling very, very alone.

"And I deserve it," she whispered to herself then wrapped up her half-eaten sandwich and stowed it away.

CHAPTER 16

Beck kept pace with her on the trip back down to the trailhead.

"What did I miss?" her friend asked.

"What do you mean?" Victoria said, still feeling the sting of Logan's abandonment. He hadn't said a word to her since he'd left her sitting alone on that damn rock.

"You both looked so happy—until you didn't. What did you do?"

Why had her friend assumed she was the one responsible? Victoria scrunched her nose. Because she knew her too well.

She glanced ahead of them to make sure Logan was far enough away he wouldn't overhear them. "I just told him the truth."

After a few moments of silence, Beck blew out

an exasperated breath. "Spill. What the hell's going on between the two of you?"

"Nothing."

"The way he looks at you isn't nothing," Beck hissed.

"We're not…compatible."

"Bullshit. You're each other's mirror image."

Victoria blinked. "What? I'm not sexist."

"Neither is he. He's protective. That goes with the territory, but so are you."

Her friend had a point, but Victoria wasn't in the mood to continue this discussion. From the look on Beck's face, she was far from through with this conversation. Victoria sighed.

"You're both stubborn as hell," Beck muttered.

If she hadn't had to keep her trekking poles tapping the ground in front of her, she would've crossed her arms over her chest. Stubborn? Seriously?

"You two slept together, didn't you?"

She shot a glare at her friend.

"I knew it!" Beck said, shaking her head. "And now, you're second-guessing yourself. You're thinking that screwing around with your partner—"

"*Shhh,*" she said, glancing around, but no one seemed to be paying them any attention.

"They can't hear us. And you're not going to avoid this conversation. You're afraid."

Victoria rolled her eyes. "I'm not afraid."

"Sure, you're not afraid of Logan or the job, but you are afraid of getting involved. You've always kept a tight lid on your emotions when you're working. Hell, it took me years to figure out you have a sense of humor."

Victoria gave a faint laugh. "It did not."

"Well, maybe that was an exaggeration, but you don't date guys you work with. That's been one of your rules for as long as I've known you, which makes it damn near impossible for you to sustain a relationship—which is ridiculous as far as I'm concerned.

"Who the fuck else would understand what your life is like? And when would you have time to be in a relationship with someone who doesn't share this life?"

Frowning, Victoria bit out, "Just because you and Roman are making it work doesn't mean we can."

Beck pressed her lips together in tight frown. "Okay. Let's look at this logically, seeing as you're getting so emotional."

"Am not," she said too quickly.

Beck arched an eyebrow.

Her cheeks heated. "Logically? How is any of this logical? Logical would be what I just did. Ending it."

Beck shook her head. "Think about it. How many more years do you intend to do this work?"

She shrugged. "As long as I am able and can contribute."

"Do you want a family?"

"I suppose. One day."

"How do you think that will happen? You're already past thirty now."

Victoria hated it when she was wrong. And she could see the flaws in her stubborn stance. "Okay, I see where you're heading with this."

"You'll be facing these decisions sooner than you want, regardless if it's Logan or some other man. But, sister, he's perfect for you."

"Logan? Perfect?" Victoria snorted.

Beck wagged her finger. "You can snort all you like, but you know it's true. Otherwise, he would never have gotten under your skin so quickly. You like him."

She more than liked him. "'Like' is not enough."

"You're right, but are you giving him—and you —a fair chance to see if this thing grows into something more?"

Feeling a little less defensive and much more dejected, Victoria cleared her throat. "It's too late. I told him I want to be reassigned to a new partner."

Beck glanced at the sky then back at Victoria. Her frown said it all, but she wasn't finished. "Well, it sounds like you need to eat some crow. Tell him how you really feel."

"But I don't know how I really feel."

Beck's gaze bored into hers. "You sure about that? I've watched the way he looks at you, but you can't keep your eyes off him either."

"That's just lust."

"Lust is a great place to start. And you like him. So, it's just a hop, skip, and a jump to love."

Victoria barked a single laugh. "A hop, skip, and a jump? You sound like my grandma."

Beck grinned. "I'm right, and you know it. Start thinking about your wardrobe."

"Good Lord, what the hell do my clothes have to do with anything?"

"Wear something sexy tonight. He won't remember what you fought about. He'll be too busy tripping over his tongue."

Victoria's jaw dropped. Her friend had never given her relationship advice before—and had certainly never encouraged her to seduce a man. "Who are you?"

Beck elbowed her side. "Your best friend. I love you, but you're an idiot."

Logan felt the walls of the room he shared with Victoria closing in around him. She was in the shower.

He hadn't spoken to her since their conversation at Delta Lake. He'd felt the need to remove himself before he said something he couldn't take back. He'd been that angry.

They'd ridden back in separate vehicles, and he'd headed straight to their room to shower first. He'd intended to be gone before she exited the bathroom, but he'd lingered, using the excuse of reviewing the feeds. They were going to meet Beck and Roman in the dining room for dinner along with the other guests. The other couple was busy showering and changing in the room Harlie had arranged for them. After that, Logan worried that Victoria would attach herself to Beck, and he wouldn't have a chance to speak privately with her until their assignment ended.

And this would likely be their last assignment together unless he could persuade her to change her mind.

But should he?

She hadn't been wrong. They'd been distracted since they'd arrived. They'd never really achieved an effective working relationship even before they'd hooked up, likely because they'd been fighting their mutual attraction from the start.

Still, he couldn't look at their time together as a mistake. He thought that if they could continue on this path, they'd find a balance. She just needed to see it through.

If she wanted to cool the physical side of their relationship, he was willing. Hell, at this point, he was all in. Whatever she needed to feel comfortable, he'd do—even let her go.

However, first, they needed to talk.

The door opened. Instead of entering the room in a towel, she was fully dressed in a sleeveless, red silk blouse and a short black skirt that hugged her hips. This time, she wore black hose with pumps rather than nude legs. Her hair wasn't falling to her shoulders but pinned up in some kind of braid that was knotted at the back of her head. She was putting up barriers. His fingers itched to pluck out the pins holding her hair up.

Her gaze was wary. "You're still here," she said softly.

He cleared his throat, not sure what to say. He didn't want her bolting from the room before they settled this. "I was hopin' we could talk about what happened today."

Her mouth tightened, but she nodded. "We have a few minutes before we'll be needed." Her gaze went to the laptop. "Harlie still in her room?"

"Yeah. Her and Adnan."

"Good.

She walked closer then stood with her hands clasped in front of her. "Look—"

"I just—" He stopped when they both started talking at the same time. "You first."

This time, she cleared her throat. "Beck said I should dress sexy, and you'd forget all about…what I said."

His lips twitched, but he didn't allow a smile. Her opening statement gave him a little hope. Someone, Beck, was on his side. "I don't think it's wise to just forget what you said. You have some issues workin' with me."

"I do." She took a deep breath. "It's not that you're not good at your job—you are."

He sighed. "But we haven't managed to keep our heads in the game."

She nodded, her eyes large in her face.

He raked a hand over his hair. "I think that will come in time. Us findin' our focus, I mean."

"I had concerns before we…" she waved a hand at the bed, "before we did that." She lifted her chin. "I'm really quite competent. I'm not sure you realize just how capable I am of being a full partner to you."

He swallowed before replying. "I'll admit, it's hard for me to stand back and let you take the lead. My natural instinct is to tuck you right behind me."

"I know. You said before you're not used to working with females, but that's your problem, not mine."

He nodded. "It is, and I can work on that. We can make this work."

"Should we?" she asked, her voice husky.

He wanted nothing more than to move toward her and wrap his arms around her, but he didn't want to spook her. "What's this really about?"

Her gaze fell away. "I've never been in this spot before…"

"You mean, fallin' for someone?" he asked softly, hoping that was where she was coming from.

Her brows lowered then relaxed again. She nodded.

That was all he needed to know. He moved toward her and opened his arms.

She took a step toward him, closing the distance.

When her head rested on his shoulder, only then did he breathe easier. "That was hard."

She gave a strangled laugh. "I've never felt more uncomfortable."

"I'd rather swallow glass than do that again," he muttered, smoothing his hands up and down her back. "We still partners?"

She nodded and leaned back to look up into his face. "Partners," she whispered. Then she lifted on her toes and kissed him.

DINNER WAS A MORE formal affair than previous nights. This was their last night together. Everyone was dressed up. Cowboys dressed in crisp snap-button shirts and new denim jeans served the guests.

Tables had been set up on the patio. Tiki torches lit. Chimineas radiated heat, but were far enough away they only took the slight chill off the air. It was comfortable. The guests had enjoyed the ranch's filet mignon dinner and were now drinking, except for the Athena Project operatives.

Beck and Roman sat at a table with Meghan and Trevor. From Meghan's pulled down mouth, she was likely disappointed their hostess looked none the worse for wear after the day's hike. Trevor's face was flushed from too much booze, and his attention wasn't glued to his girlfriend, so that was another strike for Meghan. The frowns she gave him could have curdled milk.

Elaine sat opposite and down from Harlie and Adnan. Her avid gaze crept back to the couple again and again. She was quiet but her gaze was constantly flicking over the pair.

Victoria couldn't quite figure out the woman. She seemed a bit obsessive and maybe a bit jealous of her employer, making Victoria wonder why Harlie kept her around. She figured Harlie was a little too trusting. Perhaps she'd have a conversation with her before they left to warn her that her assistant might not be someone she should put all her trust in.

And then there were Cal and Pauline. Pauline

seemed harmless, but Cal… There was something about him that rang alarm bells for her. Still, she couldn't figure out for the life of her what his motivation would be for wanting to harm Harlie or the film.

The British cowboy walked by and flashed her a smile. "Can I get you a glass of the champagne? It's really quite nice."

Victoria smiled back at him. "If I drink anything, I'll be nodding over my plate. Today wiped me out," she lied.

He nodded and moved on.

Beside her, Logan shifted in his chair. "I don't like him."

"I don't have a clue what his name is, so you know he hasn't made a big impression on me."

"It's Henry," Logan muttered. "Emmett hired him two weeks ago. It's amazin' how he's managed to be everywhere, know everything in that short amount of time."

"Hmmm." She frowned, storing away that factoid. "Last night. No one's jumping out of airplanes or zipping down mountains. Think we've weathered the worst?"

He groaned. "You know you just jinxed us, right?"

She grinned. "There are four of us keeping watch now. No one would dare come at her."

"Again," he said, patting his heart as though he was having palpitations.

Harlie stood at her table and raised her glass. "Can I have your attention?"

Conversation quieted around them. The staff moved to the outskirts of the tables, standing still so as not to distract the guests.

"I just want to thank you all for making this party so much fun. Here's to the best group of actors and film crew out there! Next week, we're going to rock!"

Cheers sounded, and glasses clinked. Harlie didn't retake her seat but moved table to table to give hugs and take selfies with her guests. When she drew near Logan and Victoria, her smile broadened. She held up her phone. "Come on, you two!"

They stood on either side of her and smiled into the camera.

After she lowered the phone, Harlie wrapped her arms around them both and squeezed. "Friends forever, you two. I hate it that you won't be on set with me next week."

"You'll be too busy to notice. And Sadie and you are going to be besties by the time the movie's in the can," Victoria predicted.

"I hope so. I really admire her. I have to admit, I'm a bit nervous."

Victoria squeezed her hand. "Sadie puts her

blue jeans on the same way you do. And she's every bit as nice as you are. You'll get along famously."

Harlie's gaze drifted to Adnan who'd moved a few feet away. His smile was soft and loving.

Victoria tilted her head toward Adnan. "He's a keeper," she whispered.

Harlie's eyes filled a little, and she blinked away the moisture. Then she leaned toward Victoria. "He proposed last night."

Victoria's eyes widened. "And...?"

She squinched her nose. "Of course, I said yes." Her gaze darted around the room. "That's just between us, though. With his family the way they are, we have work to do to make sure they won't be a problem."

Logan nodded. "That's smart."

"Well, he's rich in his own right," Harlie said. "He just has to hire the right security. I'm sure he'll be talking to Hank Patterson for some recommendations." She tilted her head. "Don't suppose you two would ever move to LA...?"

Victoria laughed. "Not a chance. Sorry. I'd love to work with you again, but I rather like the scenery around here."

"Just thought I'd ask." She gave them both a smile and walked toward Adnan whose expression was a funny mix of possessive and bemused.

"Think he knows what he's getting himself into?" Logan whispered in her ear.

"Yeah, and he's loving every minute of the chaos."

Sighing at their happiness, because she did feel a pang of envy, Victoria accepted the crooked arm Logan presented and moved with him across the patio toward Beck and Roman.

CHAPTER 17

LOGAN REMOVED his sports jacket and hung it on the chair in front of the desk then loosened his tie. "Roman is staying with the couple until they head upstairs."

"You guys are right about doing roving patrols," Victoria said. "Tonight's the last night our bad guy or guys can strike before everyone heads out tomorrow. If they're going to make a move, time's running out."

"You better change," he said, his gaze roaming over her body.

She raised a finger and wagged it. "Don't look at me like that."

"Or what?"

"Or…" she said, walking close enough her chest touched his. Slowly, she raised her arms and encircled his neck. "Or, I'll do something like this," she said and kissed him.

He groaned and placed his hands on her hips, bringing her closer so that the part of him that was always semi-horny when she was around rested against her firm belly. The kiss deepened, but before he passed that point of no return, he pulled back, turned her with his hands, and slapped her butt. "Change. Now. And wear your ugliest clothes."

She laughed as she walked away.

Twenty minutes later, they met up with Beck and Roman, who were dressed in dark clothing and boots like they were. All wore Kevlar and had holstered weapons, ready for whatever came their way—if anything was going down this night.

Victoria checked the feeds on her tablet before closing the cover. "So far, so good. All's quiet."

"We're lucky everyone called it a night, early," Roman said.

"Yeah, most of them are heading straight to the set in the morning," she replied.

"Hank has already got some Montana Protectors on the set," Beck said. "They've been keeping an eye out for any more sabotage."

"Seems everything went quiet there when Cal joined Harlie's party," Logan said.

Roman made a huffing sound. "Could be a coincidence…"

"But we don't believe in coincidences."

Beck's mouth tightened. "Swede still hasn't found anything in Cal's finances or online correspondence that would point to him being the saboteur."

Victoria nodded. "We'll still keep him top of the list for now."

"And we'll follow Harlie to the set for the hand-off," Logan said.

Beck stretched her neck to the left and then the right. "We cleared Harlie's room before heading down here. She and Adnan looked happy as clams."

"He proposed," Victoria said quietly, leaning toward Beck.

"No kidding?" Roman said, smiling. "I'm happy for them both. He seems to ground her a bit."

"Without being a helicopter-partner." Beck's gaze went to Logan, and she cleared her throat.

Logan grunted, getting her well-aimed point.

Roman pulled out a drawstring bag and emptied its contents onto his palm. They each grabbed an earpiece.

Logan flicked the switch to activate his and put it in his ear.

After they tested to make sure their comms were working, each Protector took a different side of the house to check for anything that might seem suspicious. Roman had the far side of the patio; Beck the front of the house and the far side; Victoria took the side below Harlie's window.

Logan strode down the path to the gazebo. He wanted to check out the river. It still bothered him that he'd detected someone out there the first night they'd arrived.

"All the feeds are still clear," Victoria said in his ear. "Cowboys are clearing the patio. All the hallways are empty—wait. Anita's in Harlie's corridor. She's stopped at Cal and Pauline's door. I'll keep watching."

Logan strode past the gazebo, walking softly down the path. The stars were bright above him. The sound of the river was pleasant. He was a little disappointed that Harlie hadn't planned any water activities; even fishing would've been enjoyable, although he wasn't an ardent enthusiast. Still, sitting beside the water, a cooler of beer at his feet, and Victoria sitting beside him sounded like heaven.

"Anita delivered what looks like champagne to Cal," Victoria said. "She's leaving now."

A soft thumping sounded. Not rhythmic. Hollow, perhaps metal. Curious, he walked along the river bank, heading in the direction of the sound.

He found a shallow-hulled Jon boat tied to a stump, the boat floating in the current, stretching the line, and then thumping as water forced it against the bank again. He glanced around but detected no company. Stepping closer, he saw a cluster of zip-ties tied together and left on a seat along with a black zippered bag.

When the boat hit the bank again, he leaned over and reached out, grabbing the bag from the bench, and opened it. Inside were syringes and blindfolds. "We've got a problem, guys," he said softly.

"What's up?" Beck asked.

"A boat's tied up on the river. A bag of syringes, a couple of blindfolds, and zip-ties."

"Shit. We need to get to Harlie," Victoria said.

"I'm in front. I'll go up the stairs," Beck said.

"I'm coming through the patio," Roman bit out.

"Vic, hold back," he said, then gritted his teeth because he knew she wouldn't like his order to stand down. "They'll likely take the gazebo path heading out, Vic. Stay in the woods parallel to it in case anyone gets past Beck and Roman."

He had no doubts he'd get an earful later, but for now, he made his way back through the thicket toward Victoria.

VICTORIA MADE a face in Logan's direction, but everyone on the team had their marching orders. Still holding the tablet, she cut through the trees on a path parallel to the one leading to the gazebo.

Her attention returned to the screen. "Cal's at Harlie's door. He's got the champagne and some glasses. Adnan's answering the door."

Suddenly, the feeds disappeared from her screen.

"Shit. The feeds cut out." She tossed away the tablet, preferring to keep her hands free now.

"Must've scrambled the signal. I wonder if the champagne's spiked," Beck muttered, her quickening breaths sounding in her ears. "I'm at the staircase," she added.

"Coming through the French doors, babe. Wait for me."

A huff sounded, and Victoria nearly smiled. Beck wasn't any better at "holding back" than she was.

Behind her, she heard a distant thud from the end of the house. Then two more. She paused, hiding behind a tree and staring into the dappled darkness, only stars and the crescent moon above providing any light.

Then she saw two dark figures carrying something long and cylindrical—no, a body—between them.

"They're in the woods," she whispered. "They've got her."

"Not her," Beck said, sounding winded. "Adnan. Harlie's passed out on the bed. Calling for an ambulance and backup, now. I've got her, Roman.

You head to the river." Then, "Wake up, Harlie, wake up."

"Dammit, they're heading your way, Vic," Logan said.

"I'll trail them," she whispered. "You get in front of them. Don't let them get to that boat."

"Roger," he said, his voice taut.

Moments later, she heard banging, metal on metal.

The men she followed moved faster, their low voices rising and speaking in a foreign language, but likely cursing heavily by the short terse words. One of the men dropped his end of the body they carried while the other struggled to get Adnan onto one shoulder and follow.

"One's coming your way fast, Logan," she said.

"I see him."

She heard shouts. The man in front of her dumped Adnan to the side and ran toward the commotion. "Adnan's on the ground, Roman. I've got to get to Logan."

"Roger," he said, his breaths and stomping feet sounding loud in her ear. "I'll take care of Adnan."

Victoria ran through the thicket, pushing aside vines, heading toward the sounds of fists meeting flesh. Thankfully, it appeared whoever had tried to take Adnan didn't want the sound of gunfire to alert anyone else to their plan.

The air grew cooler. Water burbled. She slowed

when she saw a shadow standing still in front of her.

Beyond the figure, Logan was fighting, his fists digging into his opponent's ribs. The figure in front of her lifted his hand. She saw the shape of a handgun. Rushing forward, she kicked out a foot, striking the back of the gunman's knee while she used her weight and momentum to take him to the ground.

His gun fired, but she quickly drew hers from the holster strapped to her thigh and ground it into the side of his cheek. "Don't move," she said, hoping the muzzle of her weapon was translation enough to tell him what she wanted him to do. He growled and froze, dropping his weapon and raising his hands off the ground.

Logan delivered one more punch, which was accompanied by the sound of bone breaking, and his opponent wilted to the ground just as Roman charged into the clearing. His glance cut from Logan to Victoria. "You all right? Did you leave me any fun?"

"Get the zip-ties off the boat," Logan said, breathing heavily. He bent and turned the man at his feet onto his stomach. When Roman returned, he quickly tied his hands and feet then pushed up from the ground to come toward Victoria who rested atop her prisoner with a hard knee pressed to his spine.

Logan kicked away the weapon the man had dropped then squatted beside Victoria. "Your move worked."

"He's not a SEAL, obviously," she said, panting.

"Let me take care of this bastard," Roman said coming up beside them. Then he waited as she pushed up from the back of the man and stepped aside.

He quickly subdued him with restraints.

In the distance, she heard sirens.

A crackle sounded in her ear. "Hey, guys," Beck said. "I heard a shot."

"Everyone's fine," Logan said. "Victoria saved my ass."

Victoria cupped a hand to her ear. "What? Say that again?"

He laughed and reached out for her, wrapping his arms around her and giving her a bear hug that squeezed the breath out of her. "That took ten years off my life."

She laughed, which came out choked sounding, and patted his shoulder. "You can let me go now."

In minutes, they were surrounded by sheriff's deputies. Half an hour later, they watched from the ranch house's front porch as a helicopter landed on the lawn, disgorging FBI agents—and Hank Patterson.

He strode toward them, his mouth stretched in

a wide grin. "I hear y'all had some excitement," he said.

"Harlie and Adnan are on the way to Jackson Memorial," Beck said, rising from her seat on the porch steps. "Harlie was already coming around when the EMTs arrived. Adnan's shoulder was dislocated when they dropped him out of Harlie's window but is otherwise fine."

"Those guys were Saudi military, sent by Adnan's former-future father-in-law," Victoria said.

Roman nodded. "They got tired of staging accidents and decided to kidnap Adnan and spirit him out of the country. Much easier and less messy than murder."

Hank shook his head. "I've got a team at the film set. We'll keep watch over the crew and have body-guards on Harlie and Adnan, but I doubt the general will try anything else now that his secret op isn't so secret anymore."

"Anita spilled the tea about the plot," Beck said. "She was paid to plant the camera but didn't know who had hired her. Tonight, she was left a cryptic note and a bottle of champagne in her car with instructions to give it to Cal. He said he'd been approached by someone claiming to represent the Saudi royal family and was paid handsomely, no questions asked, to sabotage the film set. He was assured no one would be hurt, and the money—all cash—was too good for him to say no. When Anita gave him the bottle to give to Harlie and Adnan, he realized he'd be implicated but was already in too deep to refuse."

"Both are in custody now," Roman said.

Hank nodded. "The feds are going to want to talk to them. The charges won't stay local."

His gaze swept the team. "How's this Athena Project working out for you?"

Victoria glanced at Logan.

Logan's expression didn't give away what he was thinking when he faced Hank. "I'll be the first to admit, I had concerns. I'd never worked with a female, other than in support roles. It took some adjustment—mostly of my own mindset because, in the end, Victoria's a great operative. I trust her with my back. She certainly had mine tonight."

Hank smiled as his glance fell on Victoria. "I've heard nothing but praise from Jake in the Colorado office for all the Athena Project operatives." His gaze went to Beck. "I thank you for bringing the Brotherhood Protectors this opportunity. I think we'll do a lot of good things together."

A buzz sounded, and Hank patted his shirt pocket. Pulling out his phone, he said, "I have to take this. Sadie's already at the hospital waiting for Harlie and Adnan."

As he walked away, the four teammates turned toward each other.

Roman reached out and patted Victoria's back.

"That dude looked completely embarrassed when we got him on his feet and he saw who took him down. He's not going to live that one down."

"If he returns The Kingdom, he might not live long at all," Logan said.

"Not my worry," Roman muttered. His hand went to the small of Beck's back. "It's going to be a long night. Everyone's going to want our statements. We'll be doing it in rounds—local law enforcement and the Feds. Want to go grab some coffee?"

She leaned against his side. "Sounds great." Her gaze went to Victoria and Logan. "You coming, too?"

Logan spoke before Victoria could open her mouth to respond. "We'll be along in a minute." Then he took her hand and drew her down the steps and toward the far side of the house where no one was around.

Once they were alone in the moonlight, he drew her body against his and wrapped his arms around her. When his head lowered, she sighed right before he kissed her.

After a long, heated moment, he lifted his head. "Best part of the job."

"I know, right?" she said, grinning.

"This work for you?"

"Yeah. It does."

He cleared his throat. "I wanted you in the woods. Out of the line of fire."

"I know. I wasn't waiting around for Roman while you were facing two assailants—but you didn't freak out, and you didn't lose focus. You had your guy to take down. I had mine."

"Is it bad to admit watching you in action turned me on?" he said, his voice deepening.

She laughed and pinched his side. "If it is, then I'm a sinner, too."

They kissed again, and then Logan simply held her close. Both their bodies relaxed, leaning hard into each other.

"We can have a great life," he said.

"I'd like it to be about more than just the job." She leaned back her head. "That scare you? Is it too soon?"

He kissed her forehead. "No. I like the idea of having you around, 24/7."

"As partners?" she asked, her heart beginning to thud hard inside her chest.

"Vic…" He cleared his throat. "I don't know anything about lovin' a woman, or at least I didn't before I met you. But you've been drivin' me nuts since the first day we met. You're hot as hell, every bit as stubborn as I am, and as brave as any SEAL I know." He cupped both sides of her face and rubbed his thumbs over her cheeks. "Babe, I'm fallin' for you."

Her eyes stung with tears she refused to let fall. Teary declarations weren't her style. Instead, she patted his chest and met his gaze. "Logan, I *did not* want to fall in love with you. I fought it, trying to drum up every excuse I could to prevent myself from getting involved, but…"

"I'm too irresistible, right?" he said in a teasing tone, a smile widening and his hands dropping to her hips to bring her closer. "All the right moves—"

"Just stop." She laughed, shaking her head.

His expression softened. His smile faded. "Okay, but unless you say you love me, I'm not gonna listen to another word you say."

She gulped and opened her mouth. "It's so hard…"

"I know. I get it. Sayin' those words puts it out there. There's no walkin' it back."

"You didn't exactly say it either," she said, narrowing her eyes.

He drew a deep breath. "Then here it is… Victoria Cross, I love you."

He said it so simply. Without any extra emphasis. Like it was an unalterable fact. And wasn't it the same way for her?

"I love you, Logan Tackett." And then she offered him a smile.

Slowly, his smile stretched. "Well, damn."

She chuckled. "You're such a romantic."

"You'd just roll your eyes if I got all mushy."

"Mushy?" She snickered.

"Yeah, the only time you'll let me get that way is when I'm six inches deep."

"It's gotta be seven," she muttered.

They both chuckled then suddenly, feeling giddy, she laughed out loud.

They were both grinning widely when they walked back into the ranch house to join Beck and Roman.

Beck's gaze went to their hands. Hers was enfolded by Logan's, and he wasn't letting go despite the fact his buddy Roman was smirking.

"I see you two have worked a few things out," Beck said, her tone dry.

"Yup," Logan said. "She's moving in with me."

Victoria's head whipped toward him. "I never—"

"24/7, babe."

Beck laughed. "Good Lord, I can't wait to tell the girls."

Victoria gave an exaggerated groan, but she felt happy. Somehow complete. Like the other piece of the puzzle that was the rest of her life had finally clicked into place. Life with Logan would never be boring, and they'd likely face many frustrating trials and moments of terror, but she was right where she wanted to be with the one man who was perfect for her.

"Told you," Beck said, raising her coffee cup in a mock toast.

"Well, you've been right about a lot of things," she said, then wrinkled her nose.

Logan tugged her closer to his side. "I need to call Jake."

"Yeah?" she said, glancing sideways up at him.

"We need some time off. We've got to go house-hunting."

She shook her head. He was moving fast, but that was his nature. Once his mind was made up…

"I want a dog," she blurted.

He blinked. "Okay. So, we'll need a yard." His eyes narrowed as he locked his gaze with hers. "We need two fishing poles."

She shook her head, laughing. "All right. But you're baiting my hooks."

"Done. I'd like kids someday."

"Someday, I would, too."

He gave a short, curt nod then turned back to their friends.

"That's it?" Beck said.

"Those are the important things," Logan said, then chuckled. "The rest will only be discussed when I'm six—"

"Shhh!" Victoria said, her eyes widening with alarm.

Not that Beck didn't guess what else he'd been about to say. Her wink was too sly.

Montana Bounty Hunters

Reaper (#1)

Dagger (#2)

Reaper's Ride (#3)

Cochise (#4)

Hook (#5)

Wolf (#6)

Animal (#7)

S*x on the Beach (related)

Big Sky Wedding

Quincy (#8)

Brian (#9)

Uncharted SEALs

Watch Over Me (#1)

Her Next Breath (#2)

Through Her Eyes (#3)

Dream of Me (#4)

Baby, It's You (#5)

Before We Kiss (#6)

Between a SEAL and a Hard Place (#7)

Heart of a SEAL (#8)

Hard SEAL to Love (#9)

Big Sky SEAL (#10)

Head Over SEAL (#11)

SEAL Escort (#12)

Texas Cowboys

Wearing His Brand (#1)

The Cowboys and the Widow (#2)

Soldier Boy (#3)

Bound & Determined (#4)

Slow Rider (#5)

Night Watch (#6)

Cowboys on the Edge

Wet Down

Controlled Burn

Cain's Law

Flashpoint

Triplehorn Brand

Laying Down the Law (#1)

In Too Deep (#2)

A Long, Hot Summer (#3)

Night Fall

Sm{B}itten (#1)

Truly, Madly...Deadly (#2)

Knight in Transition (#3)

Wolf in Plain Sight (#4)

Knight Edition (#5)

Night Fall on Dark Mountain (#6)

Frannie and the Private Dick (#7)

Sweet Succubus (#8)

Truly, Madly...Werely (#9)

Bad to the Bone (#10)

Long Howl Good Night (#11)

First Knight (#12)

Big Bad Wolf (#13)

Texas Billionaires Club

Tarzan & Janine (#1)

Something To Talk About (#2)

Who's Your Daddy (#3)

Love & War (#4)

Some Standalone Stories

New Orleans Nights

Begging For It

Hot Blooded

Raw Silk

Warrior's Conquest

Rogues

Enslaved by the Viking Short Story

Conquests

Smokin' Hot Firemen

ABOUT DELILAH DEVLIN

Delilah Devlin is a *New York Times* and *USA TODAY* bestselling author with a reputation for writing deliciously edgy stories with complex characters. She has published nearly two hundred stories in multiple genres and lengths, and she is published by Atria/Strebor, Avon, Berkley, Black Lace, Cleis Press, Ellora's Cave, Entangled, Grand Central, Harlequin Spice, HarperCollins: Mischief, Kensington, Montlake Romance, Running Press, and Samhain Publishing.

You can find Delilah all over the web:
WEBSITE
BLOG
TWITTER
FACEBOOK FAN PAGE
PINTEREST

Subscribe to her *newsletter* **so you don't miss a thing!**
Or email her at: delilah@delilahdevlin.com

Montana SEAL Daddy (#7)

Montana Ranger's Wedding Vow (#8)

Montana SEAL Undercover Daddy (#9)

Cape Cod SEAL Rescue (#10)

Montana SEAL Friendly Fire (#11)

Montana SEAL's Mail-Order Bride (#12)

SEAL Justice (#13)

Ranger Creed (#14)

Delta Force Rescue (#15)

Dog Days of Christmas (#16)

Montana Rescue (#17)

Montana Ranger Returns (#18)

Hot SEAL Salty Dog (SEALs in Paradise)

Hot SEAL Hawaiian Nights (SEALs in Paradise)

Hot SEAL Bachelor Party (SEALs in Paradise)

Brotherhood Protectors Colorado

SEAL Salvation (#1)

Rocky Mountain Rescue (#2)

Ranger Redemption (#3)

Tactical Takeover (#4)

Colorado Conspiracy (#5)

Rocky Mountain Madness (#6)

Free Fall (#7)

Colorado Cold Case (#8)

ABOUT ELLE JAMES

ELLE JAMES also writing as MYLA JACKSON is a *New York Times* and *USA Today* Bestselling author of books including cowboys, intrigues and para-normal adventures that keep her readers on the edges of their seats. When she's not at her computer, she's traveling, snow skiing, boating, or riding her ATV, dreaming up new stories. Learn more about Elle James at www.ellejames.com

Website | Facebook | Twitter | GoodReads | Newsletter | BookBub | Amazon

Or visit her alter ego Myla Jackson at
mylajackson.com
Website | Facebook | Twitter | Newsletter

Follow Me!
www.ellejames.com
ellejamesauthor@gmail.com